SUNDOWN TO STARDUST

WHERE SHADOW MEETS THE STAR

JAYESH SAINDANE

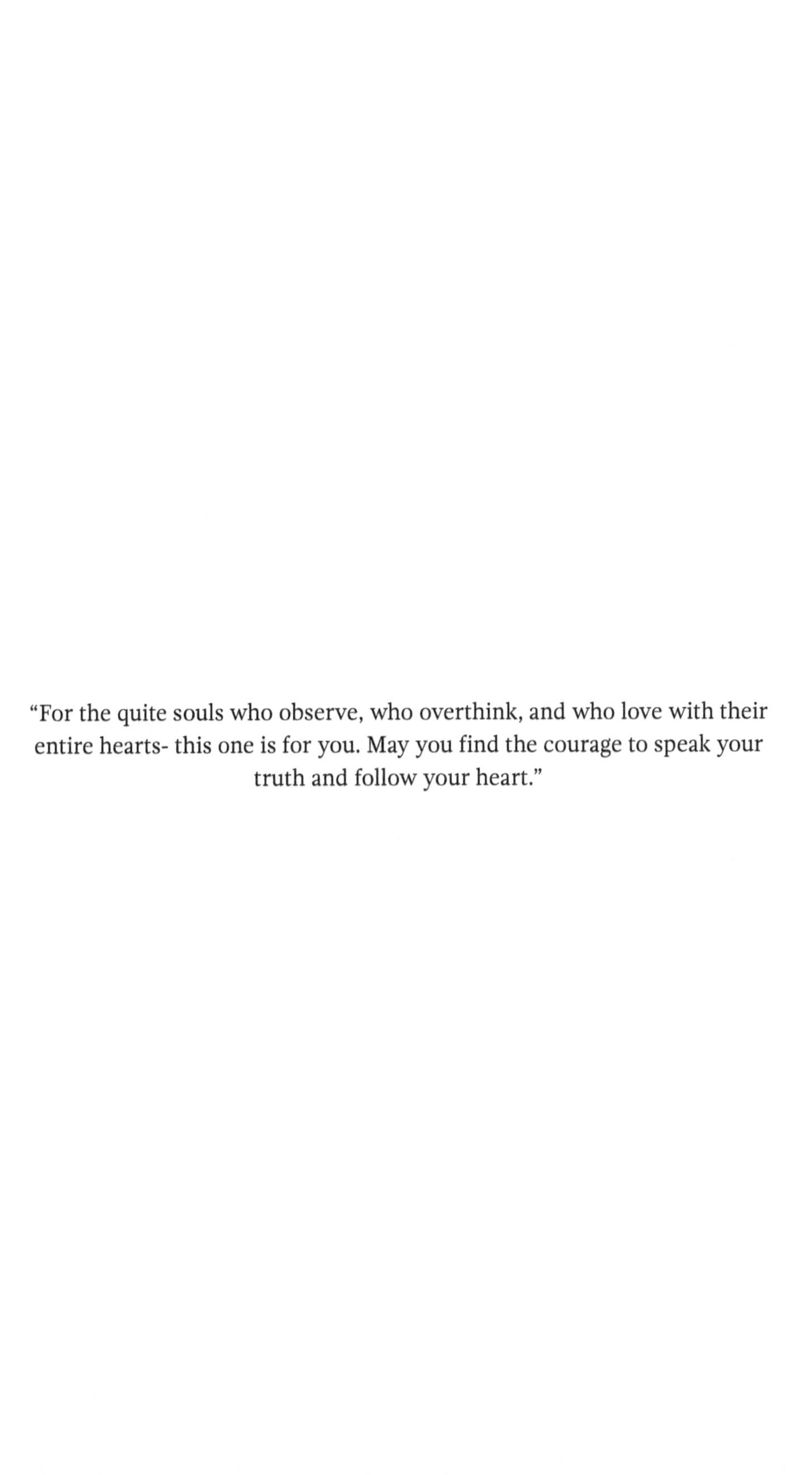

"For the quite souls who observe, who overthink, and who love with their entire hearts- this one is for you. May you find the courage to speak your truth and follow your heart."

Contents

Preface

In the world where stars and universe converge to all the intricate complexity of man, here is "Sundown to Stardust" saga of love and transformation and the relentless pursuance of dreams, set against the subtle and quaint backdrop of a small town with secrets built into its very fabric. There lies Oak Hollow and then there are Lyra and Alaric, two souls created to collide under an heavenly canopy of stars.

Lyra, the lively dreamer with an unquenchable thirst for learning, finds solace in the beauty of the night sky. Her passion for astronomy was to become a guiding light illuminating the path for her true purpose. Alaric, a being once born of darkness, deals with his newfound humanity as well as the scars from the past. Their meeting becomes serendipitous when it sparks a connection stronger than either could have foreseen.

Lyra and Alaric have to face various challenges while they are entwined in their destinies. Their love and commitment are put to the test as they experience the power of resilience through shared dreams and aspirations. They discover the depth of each other's ambitions and, together, take a journey of wonder and discovery, exploring not only the mysteries of the cosmos but also the depths of their own hearts.

It reminds one of the fact that love is something that can really make a change, make people see beyond the worlds and awaken their passions. This would be an invitation extended to the readers to take a look at the stars above and on finding the dreams they are seeking, so that they may pursue the unknown while being saturated with the bond that creates life.

Join Lyra and Alaric in this journey as they are to find their way through love and loss into infinite possibility within the constellations. In the end, this journey is not merely to know but is instead the grand celebration of that which binds us all, reminding us that in darkness lies always a light.

Prologue

In the town of Oak Hollow, whispers through ancient secrets were weaving through the trees, and the night sky was glinting with a thousand stories. It was under this vast expanse of stars, where the boundaries between light and darkness were so blurred, that two souls, destined to collide, found themselves here-now ready to be engrossed into a world where love defied odds and transformation awaited in the shadows.

Centuries had passed since Alaric had lived as one of the creatures of the night. He was imprisoned in the solitude and despair of living, with haunting memories left from a time long, long gone—a time in which he roamed among the mortals, unchained by the weight of darkness. The forest became for him sanctuary and prison both, where every rustling of leaves echoed with an ache for connection he couldn't dare hope for.

There existed Lyra, a feisty young woman whose expansiveness of dreams was of the universe itself. And so, she spent nights scanning constellations directly speaking to her heart. The stars she looked at had unknowingly been in the fate of a man who lived in the shadows. Their paths soon crossed with a chance encounter that changed the course of their lives.

Autumn leaves were falling, the crisp air carried the scent of change, and the fabric of reality began to shift. An unexpected meeting in a misty clearing would ignite a bond that did not respect time and space—a bond forged through shared dreams, whispered secrets, and a love capable of breaking even the darkest of curses.

But the deeper their connection is, the more Alaric has to face his own demons and the truth about himself that binds him to the night. They face trials and discoveries as they journey to places of old, exploring these ancient sites that would serve as keys to transformation, and the power of love capable of reshaping their own destinies.

Under the light of the stars in Oak Hollow, this is the tale of hope, love, and second chances. This is a story about the sense that even in the darkest places, love is the light that will guide us home.

STARS IN THE HOLLOW

Lyra had always felt at home under the vast expanse of the night sky. Oak Hollow, the small town she called home, was nestled between dense forests and gentle hills, where the stars seemed to shine a little brighter than anywhere else. She emerged every night from her cozy cottage, carrying her notebook and telescope with her, crossing into the woods, when streetlights went out in a small town. A narrow, one thousand times crossed for her path led the girl to a clearing seeming a secret, a one closed to the world itself. There, she found refuge in the whispers of the trees and the soft hum of the night, for stars stretched endlessly above her.

Oak Hollow was one of those small towns that belonged in another time. It was quaintly charming: a place where people knew one another, and air carried pine and earth. The main street was lined with small shops selling handmade crafts and the finest preserves. The aroma of freshly baked flaky pastries and warm bread at the local bakery wafted in each morning, and the café, which was very important to the older members, was a gathering spot for lively conversations about olden days, which ended up in laughter and memory sharing.

The buildings in Oak Hollow were painted soft, fading colors; the facades were worn, with years of weather and time. Every shop and home had its stories, whispers of love and loss, celebration and sorrow. Lyra wandered these streets often during the day, lost in the rhythm of the town. But with all the warm smiles and friendly nods from townsfolk, she never quite felt like she belonged. For an instant, it was almost as if she were some aimless traveler wandering through but cannot yet say why. Except in the woods, perhaps, for in the forest, she was different--as if exactly where she was, exactly what was meant to be.

There was the sanctuary of this clearing on the edge of the forest, where perhaps the sky would open its expanse like nowhere back in town ever did with a view that painted her constellations by rote. She would set up her telescope, focusing its power with a delicate hand. Then she would back onto the cool grass and allow the night to engulf her. Orion, Cassiopeia, and Draco filled her view, yet she was always searching for more. Every star twinkled in promise, every constellation promised a story. She wished to discover a new star or constellation, leave her mark on the universe, that was always beyond her. She looked up, her mind's eye imagining that she floated among those bright lights, free from loneliness, which clung to her like a shadow.

Lyra's loneliness was a quiet thing, to slide in during the pauses between townspeople conversations or when she caught herself staring blankly at her reflection in a shop window. She wanted something: an attachment, something deep that could be likened to the stories the stars told her every night. There were the familiar rhythms in the heartbeat of Oak Hollow, but her heart danced to the beat of a different kind of rhythm, one of echoes of the cosmos. She longed to find someone who understood the pull she felt toward the mystery of the night sky and somebody who might see in twinkling lights the same wonder. But for the night, she was alone in her small world, with all the constant, comforting feeling of the stars around her.

The moon, the next night, hung bright. It had become full once more and cast silver shadows among the trees while lighted up the clearing itself. Lyra laid herself back on the cool earth, and the night breeze danced through the leaves in caressing fingers. She opened her notebook, which was full of star and constellation drawings and night-time notes that filled page after page. With each stroke of her pencil, she brought the heavens closer to her, translating the language of the cosmos into something tangible, something she could hold onto.

As she sketched, her mind would wander off to the dreams she had of being an astronomer. She saw herself standing at a grand observatory, with fellow stargazers sharing discoveries that could change how humanity understood the universe. But those dreams seemed as far away as the stars themselves. Oak Hollow and its traditions and expectations always seemed to pull her back when she dared to reach for something more. It was a place where everything seemed set in place, people stayed, and adventures were confined to the pages of books.

Yet, despite that heavy burden of expectation, there still flickered within her some hope in the heart. Somewhere far out over the horizon was a world waiting for her. Maybe someday she'd be out of the small confines of Oak Hollow chasing after those stars. She'd probably find herself, one of these days, destined to be as huge as all those stars which she loved.

She sat up suddenly, her heart racing at the rustling in the underbrush. She half-expected to see a deer or some other forest creature darting across her line of vision. But the night was silent, except for the distant hoot of an owl. She shook off the unease and turned her gaze back to the sky, determined not to let anything disturb her peace.

But as she turned back to her stargazing, a shiver ran through her. It was then that she saw something - a streak of light shooting across the sky, brighter than any shooting star she could have ever seen. Lyra took her breath in as her fingers traced the path it took, and a thrill of possibility shot through her. It was beautiful, and fleeting glimpse of something, some fleeting glimpse of things that had eluded her grasp. She couldn't help but wonder if maybe it was some sign.

The light was no more transient than it seemed. Only a sense of wonder lingered. "Maybe it's a comet," she whispered to herself, thinking on possibilities. Maybe it was the discovery she hoped to make, maybe something extraordinary was just beginning. She ran with some scribbled notes, her hands shaking with excitement. The loneliness was over, at least, as if a possibility's thrill replaced it.

As she dismantled her telescope and covered her notebook, the moon began to set, lowering the world into deeper hues of twilight. Lyra stayed for a moment or two longer, not wishing to let the enchantment of the night slip beyond her. But the cooling air nipped at her nose and reminded her of the coming dawn, full of obligations and expectations with another day in Oak Hollow.

Till next time, she said to herself, then glanced at the stars for the last time. She started backing off from the clearing, her heart made light by the little fire that burned on it, which had been ignited by that shooting star.

Walking home tonight felt different, with the prospect of adventure within every step taken with quiet determination that would perhaps help her reach for something extraordinary. The twinkling stars above knew full well, encouraging her to dream bigger, to go higher, and never look back on what lay ahead.

She had reached her cabin, where warm familiarity surrounded her and she was yet outside herself and embracing the night. But Lyra's heart began to fill with this sense of faith in what living in Oak Hollow stood for: just the beginning in the boundless expanse of the universe, about finding connections that would become a part of her as the stars filled up the sky.

She tucked her notebook under her pillow, smiled, closed her eyes, and dreamed of distant galaxies and the adventures that awaited her. The night sky was not a backdrop but a canvas for her dreams, reminding her that she was destined for more than the confines of a small town. And somewhere in that expanse, she felt certain that her story was just beginning.

CHAPTER TWO

Eyes in the Shadows

Alaric moved through Oak Hollow like a ghost, always keeping to the edges, always preferring the quiet solitude of the woods. His cabin, hidden deep among the trees, was a place he rarely left. It was a small, weathered structure, surrounded by towering pines and tangled underbrush. Inside, it was bare bone bare, bed, wood stove, some shelves full of dusty books which stood against the walls like mute companions. Each tome was the last remainder of a life once lived and in those words lie faintly an echo of joy, sorrow, and adventure. It was there where Alaric could keep his peace from townfolks' chattering lips and probing eyes. He had grown accustomed to loneliness, the way it blanketed him like a mantle, shielding him from a world that never seemed inviting in the first place.

Down deep in the forest he had constructed a life-only simple, regulated by simple rules. He rose with dawn to tend his small garden - a patch of earth wildflowers mixed with herbs and vegetables. He would spend his days collecting firewood, fishing in the nearby stream, or losing himself in the pages of the books that had become his lifeline. The world outside his cabin continued to turn, the seasons changed, but within his secluded sanctuary, time felt suspended, marked only by the shift of the sun and the phases of the moon.

But that all changed the night he saw her.

It was a coincidental meeting because he would so often get lost in wandering along the woods, his soul clearing of all morasses and reviving thoughts. Such was filled with sounds produced by creatures at no time, though his heart and mind carried the heaviness of something weighing upon the two. Amidst moving unnoticed among those trees, ahead from where the light stood little, an illumination existed between the wood darkness - perhaps a spark to a lost soul who was attracted closer for answers.

He was so intrigued that he crept noiselessly forward, dodging among the trunks to avoid stirring up too much noise. Damp earth smell and pine fill the air as he moves to the border of this clearing. And there, lost beneath the stars, was Lyra.

He couldn't tear himself away from her view, captivated by the way it looked as though she owned the night, with features wide open and wonder inside, something he had forgotten long ago. The fireworks of stars enlightened her eyes that had a magical beauty, something ethereal, almost an otherworldly being. Alaric felt something stirs in his chest, a yearning he hadn't felt for years—a sense of want, of slight pain, that he could not explain. He had the sense of looking upon a world from which he'd long strayed.

She reminds him of things he once loved about the world: its beauty, especially the stories that patterns hold in the stars, thrill of discovery every celestial thing brought. More than those, she reminded him how it felt to care about someone other than himself, to be curious.

He saw her writing notes in a notebook as old as she was; the furrow on her brow showed how she wrote those notes. She paused now and then to glance at the stars through her telescope, her eyes flashing bright with excitement as she discovered all the wonders of the night sky. He somehow found comfort in her presence; he hadn't felt as connected to another human being in years. He felt that he was looking through a window into an existence he had longed for so long ago: full of passion and purpose, and empty of the shadows that clung to regret.

Day by day, and yet more so night by night, Alaric would return to the clearing like a moth to flame, memorizing the pattern in which she gazed up toward the stars, committing each constellation to memory that glimmered above. He listened to her soft murmurings as she addressed the night, telling it of her thoughts and asking its opinion upon the stars. He longed to go to her, to join in her wonder at this place of moon and dream.

But Alaric was a man with the past etched on him like scars; it had taught him to keep other people at a distance. He carried the weight of old secrets, memories that haunted him in the quiet moments when he let his guard down. In the solitude of his cabin, the echoes of his history reverberated through the silence, each whisper a reminder of the mistakes he had made and the people he had lost. He fears what will happen if he allows someone like Lyra close to him again, opens himself up to feeling something. Therefore, he lives in the shadows, even though a part of him craves stepping out into the light.

As the sun dipped over the mountains, Alaric began to consume himself under fascination with her presence, observing those little things of life-the way moonbeams brushed through her hair, the way laughter rang through the rustling of fallen leaves, and how, closing her eyes, drawing a deep draught she seemed to inhale-all cosmic essence about her, seemed to find its places inside his memory as a poignant reminder of what he could no longer possess.

But there were times when the darkness seemed almost to envelop him, times when he felt the tug of his own history clawing at his heart. He would find himself sitting alone in his cabin, the shadows creeping closer, and the weight of solitude would settle upon him. The silence was oppressive, and he would close his eyes, desperate to drown out the past. But even in such dark hours, the mere thought of Lyra came as a flicker of light, a beacon from which he was saved falling into despair.

On a certain night, the anticipation was so thick in the air that the stars gleamed like diamonds scattered across velvety blackness. Alaric had an uncharacteristic boldness to venture out into that clearing once more. The rustling of leaves was soft, and the nocturnal calls were soft as he passed through the woods. Every night, he found the path more familiar, but his chest still ached from all the walls he had constructed around himself.

He finally reached the clearing and stopped at the edge of it, taking in what he saw before him. Lyra sat on the grass, her body outline marked by the silvery light of the moon. She was drawing intently, her pencil racing across the page, drawing forth the splendor of the cosmos that made Alaric's heart leap in his chest. He just stood there for a moment, simply watching as the view before him. And then the world around faded off, leaving the two of them, one in love with the green tree-tops all above him, the other with the brown shadows under the trees.

But then, as if feeling his presence, Lyra looked up, her eyes searching the clearing. Alaric held his breath in the moment of fear and hope. Would she see him? Would she feel something of the connection that brought him to her? Stepping back into the dark, he watched until noticing a glimmer of surprise in her eyes.

"Hello?" she whispered loudly, her voice full of gentleness and resolve, yet still clear, even in the night darkness. Alaric's heart thumped hard; he wished to step forward yet shunned to emerge, to appear. He was so sensitive to her regard scanning through the dark. She could sense the excitement, wonder emanating from her, that drove her questions.

Alaric hesitated, his conflicting desires causing him to struggle. Finally, he stepped forward and emerged into the light. The moment was surreal, like a dream in which reality and fantasy blurred. "It's just me," he replied in a low, rough voice from disuse.

Lyra's face changed, surprise giving way to cautious interest. "You've been watching me, haven't you?" No accusation in her voice-only curiosity, a genuine desire to understand.

"I—" he started to say, but the words dried in his mouth. He had not expected her to face him, to see beyond the darkness he had draped around himself. He had not expected her to move forward, into the moonlit clearing where their two worlds stood starkly opposed.

"I didn't mean to intrude," he whispered, barely above a breath. "I was drawn to your light."

Her eyes lit up with a knowledge that cut through all the walls he'd erected around himself. "My light?" she repeated, her head cocked slightly. "You mean the stars? Or me?"

"Both," Alaric said, feeling naked under her scrutiny. "You.you have a way of looking at the universe I've forgotten."

Lyra's expression softened, and a gentle smile played on her lips. "It's easy to forget when you're surrounded by darkness."

He nodded, feeling suddenly exposed as if she had caught sight of the raw core of his being. "I've been in shadows so long, I'm not sure I know how to step into light."

"Perhaps it is time you try," she said, her voice full of encouragement yet tinged with compassion. "The stars are beautiful, but they are nothing without someone to share them with.".

Her words awakened something inside him, which he thought had long been buried deep. For perhaps the first time in years, he felt a flutter of hope, a promise of connection that welcomed him forward. Under the vast expanse of the night sky, he finally realized that he was no longer alone.

As they stood together in the clearing, two souls touched by the stars, Alaric felt the weight of his past begin to lift. The shadows that had clung to him for so long began to fade, replaced by the warmth of Lyra's presence.

In the middle of his loneliness, he had discovered a soul mate, a reminder that even the darkest nights could be lit up by the light of another.

From that night on, their lives began to overlap in a manner that was quite not his idea. Often during nights when stars adorned the sky, Alaric would share the story of his life, along with the dreams and hopes it bore for him. When he talked of Lyra's love for astronomy and the fire she seemed to feel in that field, something he could not ignore in those stars was rekindled. In turn, bits and pieces of his old days were discussed by Alaric with her- -burdens, and the experience gathered from many lonely years.

With each visit, Alaric opened himself up with every crack that allowed light in. He started telling tales of love for the forest and the beauty of wildness cradling him from as long as he can remember. Lyra listened keenly with wide eyes full of wonder at the pictures painted in his words, ancient trees whispering their secrets, rivers like veins running through the land.

As she opened his eyes to the universe beyond, there were the mysteries of the stars, the stories that they had to tell, and she took him across into the unknown depths of night, seeing the light reflected in constellations which lit the darkness. He knew their names-their importance, their myths-and within every tale he found bits and pieces of himself returned back.

But with each step forward, Alaric's fear of it growing stronger, the lines of their bond shadowed his past-the man he once was. His revulsion would assail him constantly-the dark legacy that had defined his existence and all that he kept hidden.

Yet, seeing the wonder and warmth filling her eyes, he perceived a glimmer of hope. Maybe this time was different. Maybe love could ignite transformation, become a strength powerful enough to dispel for him the darkness that has defined him for so many years.

It had grown quiet with autumn's arrival in Oak Hollow; nights now drew out endlessly and starlight blazed into flame as the seasons finally changed.

Alaric stepped back from the edge of the clearing one night as he watched Lyra arrange the telescope. Crisp autumn air filled the senses: fallen leaves' earthy scent promising something to be different.

"Alaric!" she shouted enthusiastically. "Come and take a look!"

He couldn't help but step forward, drawn into the light that shot out from her. "What is it?" he said, not looking at her.

"Just look!" she urged, her eyes sparkling.

As he peered through the eyepiece, his breath caught in his throat. The view before him was breathtaking—a cluster of stars swirling in a kaleidoscope of colors, a celestial dance that seemed to pulse with life.

"It's beautiful," he breathed, feeling a sense of wonder wash over him.

Isn't it?" she replied, standing beside him, their shoulders brushing lightly. "Each one has its own story, its own place in the universe. Just like us."

And there, in her words, Alaric felt a shattering as the walls he had raised began to crumble, and for the first time in all the years he had wandered, the shadows that pursued him could not stand up against the light they'd created together.

"Perhaps," he said slowly, "it's time for me to tell you my story."

Lyra looked at him without wavering, her gaze full of understanding. "When you're ready, Alaric. I am here.".

As he stood there beside her, the weight of his past still lingered on, but for the first time, he felt that flicker of hope being ignited in his heart - a chance to embrace the light, to step out of the shadows, and to share not just his story, but his life with her.

And with this realization, Alaric knew he was ready to take the first step into the light.

CHAPTER THREE

THE STRANGER AND THE STARS

Lyra sat as usual, deep in the clearing. Her spine ran chill; there was a part of her that told her she wasn't alone. She glanced around at the edges of the clearing. Shadows lurked, but she couldn't see anything else. The forest was quiet, except for the crunching of leaves in the wind. Yet, she couldn't stop feeling as though she were being watched. Oddly, she didn't fear it; instead, an odd sense of curiosity consumed her, a feeling that something- or someone-was out there, hidden just beyond her sight.

Low on the horizon, the moon cast a silver glow in the clearing where it brightened the wildflowers and the ferns swaying delicately in the wind. Wrapping her arms about her knees, Lyra let her heart race with the thought of a visitor; maybe it was only a deer or a raccoon that was curious to come near, she kept repeating to herself, but this instinctive urge of curiosity made her want to be on her guard.

Then came a snap of a twig behind her. The sound boomed out in the stillness like a clap of thunder. She felt a jump of fear as her eyes met a figure stepping into moonlight. He was tall and lean, his clothes merged with the darkness, and the face was hidden by the brim of a worn hat. He wears the shadows like an old friend; they cling him and look at each other, a silent pause hung between them like a slack, tight string.

Surprised mixed in with intrigue wash over Lyra. The stranger, while unmoving to the stir of life, seemed to possess some kind of magnetism there as if his stillness ordered her attention like never she had felt it before. Alaric stands forth before her. The two urges: withdraw from hiding in the shadow into hiding and the other mysterious urging of her own gazeful attention.

Who are you?" she asked, her voice breaking the stillness that enveloped them. The question hung in the air, echoing in the vastness of the night.

The man hesitated, uncertainty flickering across his features, but he shook his head, his gaze lingering on her telescope before drifting back to the sky. "I'm not from around here," he finally replied, his voice low and gravelly, a hint of melancholy threading through his words.

Lyra followed his gaze; a flicker of recognition passed between them, an acknowledgment that they both shared, unspoken, a passion for the stars. Neither am I, she found herself saying, curiosity on her face. But often I come here to watch the stars. They remind me of how vast the universe is, how small we are.

He studied her seriously, and his chest pounded wildly within him; still, still, he wanted to hear more. "I've mapped the constellations," she continued, speaking over the stillness in a whisper. "I was trying to catch their beauty in my drawings.".

For a moment, a spark of interest flickers to life in the somber depths of his eyes. "What do you see?" he asks in a softer tone as he takes a step closer to her.

"Hope," she answers with confidence, feeling a sense of courage for herself. "A connection to something greater than ourselves. It's like the stars carry all the stories of the world, waiting for someone to listen.".

There, silent, for a moment with the weight of shared wonder suspended in the air. He stood there, his gaze cast upon her, the depths of his thoughts sensed; shadows of his past dancing behind his eyes. "What's your name?" she asked, breaking the spell that held them captive.

"Alaric," he said simply. "And you?

Lyra. The name seemed to promise a ritual incantation. An adventure was brewing inside. She stretched forward, and he took her hand cautiously, as if she were about to shatter that delicate moment of time hanging between them.

A spark of electricity shot through her at the spot where their hands touched; yet, it was more of an ancient and deep sensation, as if souls found each other from years beyond memory. She saw, in his eyes, how uncertain he was; behind the mask of invulnerability, a flicker of vulnerability.

Slowly he released her hand, pulling back a little as though the touch burned him. Old fear crept into his heart, and he could feel an urge to retreat before he says too much. "I should leave," he whispered low.

"No," Lyra encouraged softly but firmly. "Stay a little longer. Talk about the stars.".

He paused, his eyes sliding toward the shadows of the forest, the memories of his past tugging at him. But something in Lyra's eyes held him, and he was drawn back into the clearing's light. "I don't know much," he said, and it was almost as if admitting it released the tension between them.

Then let's learn together," she suggested, bubbling over with enthusiasm. "There is an entire universe outside to explore."

Alaric nodded, with a hesitating smile, his dark past still weighing upon him, but it felt less overwhelming under the warmth of her being. They settled on the cool earth of the soft grass as they gazed upward toward the night sky.

Do you see that constellation?" she asked, pointing out at a group of stars sparkling brightly over their heads. "That's Orion. He is a great hunter in the night. They say it's on account of being so wonderfully handsome that even the huntress goddess loved him down to her depths.".

Alaric listened intently as she weaved tales of celestial being and mythological stories around the voice of magic carried through the air. Then there were the Seven Sisters, the Pleiades, and how they travelled the cosmos. She connects the beauty to the act of connection with the bonds that live forever.

Did you know the stars we see are all ancient light?" she'd ask, her eyes sparkling with excitement. "Some of them may no longer be there, and yet, here we stand, beholding their warmth.".

Alaric looked at it in a manner no other could; the wonder to her view of life; "It's beautiful" he whispered, as something was stirring inside of him; "Like ghosts from yesteryears past, reminding us what may never come again". she burst with excitement "That's right! Like everyone! Everyone is part of such an extensive tapestry in life; all joined into each other by tales and reminiscences.".

They told stories of constellations in the night, but much more besides. They talked about their lives: Lyra's dreams of becoming an astronomer, traveling to distant places to study the stars up close, and Alaric's lingering shadows, the memories that haunted him in the quiet moments.

"Why do you hide away in the woods?" she asked gently, her gaze steady and inviting.

Alaric shrugged. The weight of everything weighed him down. Finally, he admitted, "I... lost my way". Those words tasted bitter inside his mouth.

"I wanted to escape it by withdrawing into the shadows as it seemed like the key out, but now that was not the answer".

Lyra nodded, having a very understanding expression in her face. "Sometime it is easier for hiding than facing what was inside. But you cannot do it alone.".

Her words just hung there, a lifeline offered to him in the dark. He felt the warmth of her presence, how she drew him out of the confinement of his past. "Thank you," he said whispering, his heart swelling to mixture of gratitude and vulnerability.

Night grew darker; a celestial blanket of twinkling stars would shine across to illuminate the clearing, the night a little lighter at its bottom. Hope lighted deep within the void of his heart and became a light that made everything around seem brighter to his eyes, or Alaric seemed to have felt so with himself.

But when the first light of dawn crept into the sky, casting a soft lavender and gold glow across the horizon, Alaric knew he had lingered too long. The old fear began clawing at him once again, the instinct to retreat rising to the surface. "I should go," he said reluctantly, rising to his feet. "Before I overstay my welcome.".

Lyra stood too, with a shadow of disappointment about her features. "Are you coming back?" she questioned, and her voice rose to a soft plea in this question, pulling hard upon his heart.

He thought for a moment then dropped his eyes to her, drawn on that earnest face. "I will," he told himself, his words ringing on him as weight; his voice was rough and final - "I want to".

Alaric turned his head back at the stars and then retreated into the shadows as the call of the forest drew him back home. As he disappeared into the darkness, he could feel Lyra's presence there, like the dying glow of the stars, leaving behind a warmth in the air that clung to their connection.

Left alone in the clearing, Lyra thought of the stranger. Who was he? What story hid behind those sad eyes? She felt a depth about him, a complexity, and wondered what secrets this forest might hold and if Alaric was part of them.

For the next several nights, she returned to the clearing. She couldn't get the stranger that she had met under the stars out of her mind. The woods were changed; they were alive now with possibility. She ached for answers to all the questions that swirled in her mind.

And then, one evening, as she settled into her spot with her telescope, she felt a familiar presence in the air. The anticipation coursed through her veins, and her heart quickened as she turned to see Alaric stepping cautiously into the clearing once more.

"Hello, Lyra
," he said, his voice a soft murmur, filled with the weight of unspoken thoughts.

"Alaric," she said, and a smile crossed her face like the dawn. "I was hoping you'd come back."

He came closer, his heart being pulled toward the warmth of her presence, which engulfed him like an impenetrable protective shield. "I couldn't stay away," he said, with all the sincerity of it making her heart flutter.

They spent the night telling stories and laughter as the stars looked over them, their own little world deepening as the hours went by. The shadows that had held to him for so long receded as the light that Lyra brought upon the hidden corners of his heart seemed to come back.

And the night passed, with their comfort in each other. Every moment they shared took them closer to one another. Lyra's laughter echoed through the clearing and wove a tapestry of warmth where shadows that clung to Alaric once hid.

He knew the shadows of his past would always be there, but he found new strength in life with Lyra. They journeyed into the depth of their stories together, and every revelation brought them closer to the light that was waiting for both of them.

Above him twinkled the stars as he realized that perhaps he was finally home, not in the woods but in some place in his heart that could be home, to a place where he would embrace the unknown with somebody who understood the beauty of both light and shadow.

And as night fell, they looked up to the stars, their hearts beating together under the watchful eye of the stars, two souls dancing together in a dance of fate, where each step would bring them closer to the truth for which they had both been searching

CHAPTER FOUR

ACHING HEARTS

The nights turned chilly, but Alaric returned to the clearing for reasons that had little to do with habit and everything to do with a need he hadn't felt in years. The air was now crisp, filled with the scent of fallen leaves, and the forest was quiet; it was Lyra's presence that warmed him. For as much as she represented - in all her confusing complications-a source of comfort in some aspects, a shine bright within the darkness of being surrounded, or perhaps even immersed into for such a very long time. And a steadily building attachment terrified him; for so long had he told himself that aloneness was better. All this isolation was like the ultimate shield: protection from what of himself he'd only never fully be able to be in control of. But with Lyra, the walls were beginning to crack.

Every night, the stars twinkled above them like watchful guardians, their constellations casting a light that illuminated not only the clearing but the corners of Alaric's heart he thought long forgotten. As he watched Lyra share her passion for the cosmos, her eyes sparkling with excitement, he felt an ache that was both beautiful and painful. He had seen many stars in his old age, but no one had ever looked at the stars with such a love-lorn gaze in his lifetime.

Lyra felt the change in Alaric's mood. She felt that his eyes lingered a little longer on her, and how his voice softened as he spoke to her, though the words were still measured. Shadows in his eyes were not so easy to overlook. He had opened up to her in ways she had not expected, yet there was a barrier, a secret he could not bring himself to share.

And in those nights when they would sleep side by side, she'd turn to him, seeking answers to her questions about wanting to drag out of his shell the man in Alaric. "What do you see when you look up at the stars, Alaric?" she'd ask with a mischievous undertone, trying to elicit a faintest glimmer of a smile from him. And he would always answer her with a thoughtful look on his face, considering not just the cosmos but the meaning of their bond itself.

"I see stories," he'd say, his voice heavy, laced with something more, something beneath the surface. "Every star holds a tale, a piece of history."

"Like us?" she'd suggest, caught by the depth of his words. "Our own story written among them?"

He'd nod to respond, but his eyes would always show the shadow of sadness as if he could feel the weight of unsaid stories against his chest. The connection was genuine, and he loved holding it close, yet he's scared of what might lie below the surface and could swallow him whole.

His past followed him like a shadow and remained with him most times. It was a secret that he carried around, kind of like a scar. Alaric had learned long ago not to tell people too much about himself lest it brought disaster upon him. He had remembered the turned faces with fear, and the voices became cold once they knew of what he was capable. And now with Lyra, he dreaded history repeating. He would hate to make her suffer or to find his truth diminishing the radiance of light in her eyes. Every time he looked into her eyes, he felt the urge to be honest, to bare things he had buried so deep. Yet the thought of losing her, of watching that spark fade, sent chills through him. The fear that gripped him was suffocating; he could no longer distinguish between the longing to be close to her and the terror of being discovered.

There were nights when Alaric stood at the edge of the clearing, the moonlight making the path ahead. He would pause, heart thumping, and turn away into the shadows. It was on those nights that he vanished that left this strange ache in Lyra's chest, an aching hollow that surprised her. Standing alone in the clearing and staring up at the stars, she felt as though his absence had opened some kind of physical wound within her.

'Come back', she would be whispering to the winds sometimes hoping them to carry her words in to him. She still didn't confront him whenever he came back, as any show of this would hurt, but the feeling of his non-return had stayed there itself like a guest one disliked. Each time she did catch sight of his fading shadow slipping into the trees, she feared he won't return.

When with her, Alaric seemed to make her feel seen and treasured, understood.

They talked of stories and laughter and of dreams under starry skies, but with every passing day, the distance he pushed on in silence weighed heavy on her heart. She felt the battle going on inside him-the turmoil he tried to keep hidden. Lyra had always assumed it was the love and connections with other people that granted individuals all this power, but trust in vulnerability that is equal to strength. But this she hadn't lost a deep faith and still not; yet now began the feeling of creeping doubts and edges. One evening, the moon hung low in the sky and cast a silvery glow over the clearing. Lyra had brought her telescope, wanting to share the wonders of the universe up close with Alaric. She set it up, her fingers shaking as she adjusted the lens to find a view she wanted to share with him.

"Look at that," she said excitedly, her eyes sparkling as she pointed at a group of stars. "Isn't it beautiful? Just consider all the stories that the fabric of space weaves with its tapestry."

Alaric took a moment, his heart racing as he watched her eyes light up with wonder. He wanted to be part of that excitement, share in that joy, but what lay hidden within him created a storm of turmoil within his chest. He felt the weight of her gaze; the way she looked at him was as if he were the stars themselves: bright and full of potential.

"It is beautiful," he finally said, his voice barely above a whisper.

"Come on, look through the telescope! I want to show you," she insisted, practically bouncing with enthusiasm. She adjusted it again, coaxing him closer.

He advanced slowly, his heart beating in his chest. Gazing through the lens, he was amazed at the play of the stars and that something of the sense of wonder reminded him of the joys he had long abandoned. But under that joy lay a deep-rooted fear that reminded him of the darkness that lingered just beyond the edges of his memory.

"It's incredible," he said, grinning, but Lyra saw a flicker of something darker in his eyes.

"Imagine," she mused, "travelling through space, exploring worlds beyond our own." She turned to him, shining with hope. "Imagine what it would be like if we could do that someday?"

Alaric could feel the warmth of her enthusiasm embracing him, but that the idea of such dreams tore a heart-aching mix of longings and despair through him. "That's far away," he said, in the attempt to temper down the excitement she was inflicting upon him.

"Maybe," she said, gently dropping her gaze onto the ground. "We can make it happen, don't you think?

He wanted to tell her yes, to reassure her that dreams were within reach, but the truth felt like a jagged knife in his gut. He kept quiet, stuck between the worlds of her dreams and his reality.

His unspoken words between them were deafening. Lyra realized a change in his expression-the smile faltered on him and the gaze became rather remote. "Alaric," she began tentatively, "what is wrong?"

"Nothing, I tell you," he replied quickly, his gaze moving elsewhere.

"Don't lie to me," Lyra sternly replied, crossing her arms over her chest. "I can see that. You are not really here.".

He shifted uncomfortably, feeling the walls he had built around his heart closing in on him. "I'm just... thinking."

"I am thinking about what," she pressed, determination etched on her features.

He shrugged. "About everything. About how things might be different, how I might be different. About the future."

Her heart was racing at the import of his words. "You mean our future?

Yes," he said, finally looking at her. "But I can't. Not the way you deserve."

"Why not?" she asked, her voice quivering. "What's holding you back? You're not just a shadow of your past, Alaric. You can be more.".

He swallowed hard, his secrets aching in his chest. "What if I can't be that person you want me to be? What if I'm too broken to ever be put back together?"

Lyra came closer, her heart breaking for him. "You're not broken. You're human, just like me. You've made mistakes, but who hasn't? We all have shadows in our past.".

"Not like mine," he returned, the vulnerability in his voice laced with fear. "I carry things that could ruin everything, Lyra. I'm not who you think I am."

The racing of her heart became more pronounced as uneasiness settled in the pit of her stomach. "So tell me the truth then. Let me help. Please don't shut me out.".

His heart reacted to the desperation in her voice, yet he went deeper into darkness. "I can't. You won't understand what I did. What I am."

He leaned into her face. "I want to understand," she said again, her eyes searching for answers in his. "You have opened up in so many ways. Trust me with this.".

He didn't let them spill out. They bubbled inside him, a volcanic eruption ready to burst free. But fear of losing her kept them contained. "Lyra, please. Just know that whatever you think I am, it's far from the truth."

. . .

The ache in her chest expanded and a familiar sense of loss crept in. "You're scaring me, Alaric. I don't want to lose you.".

"You won't lose me," he said, the desperation seeping into his voice. "But I can't be what you want. I can't give you what you deserve."

The silence that followed was deafening, a chasm that seemed to stretch between them, filled with unspoken words and unanswered questions. Lyra could feel the tears pricking at her eyes, but she refused to let them fall. "I just want to be there for you," she whispered, her voice barely audible. "I care about you, Alaric. More than you know.".

His heart twisted painfully as she spoke. "And that's the problem," he said, his voice thick. "The more you care, the more it hurts."

Lyra stepped back, a shuddering breath caught as she tried to take on the weight of his confession. "You can't push me away. I won't let you."

He broke, his voice rough and raw. "I have to. For your own good."

"Then let me decide what's good for me," she snapped, frustration laced with desperation. "I'm not afraid of your past. I want to know you, all of you."

"Knowing me could cost you everything," he warned, his eyes dark with emotion.

"I'm willing to take that risk," she declared, her resolve hardening. "You've already taken a piece of my heart, Alaric. I can't walk away now."

For a moment, Alaric froze as walls he had constructed around his heart shook at her words. The warmth of her presence was calling to him to take that step closer toward the edge of vulnerability that he had long avoided.

But then, as he looked at her eyes brimming with a sense of purpose and some glimmer of hope, the fear returned in his chest. He could still see the shadowy reminder of his existence: its consequences.

"I can't," he whispered to her in broken murmurs.

Lyra's heart crumbled to pieces at the stdefeat. "Why?"

Because I do not want to see you hurt," he said, his voice full of emotion. "You deserve a life free from my darkness. I can't risk pulling you into my world."

"You are not a monster," she said, her voice steady despite the ache in her heart. "You are a man, with fears and scars, just like everyone else. We can face this together.".

"I don't know how to be together," he whispered barely. And then his voice got too low.

"Then let's learn," she prodded, her heart throb with anguish, urging closer. "I'm not afraid of the unknown. I just need you to meet me halfway."

Tears welled into her eyes, and another step she took forward. She was closing in on him now. "Please, Alaric, let me understand. Let me help you heal,"

For the first time, the dam within Alaric begins to crack. His past pains met with her warm words against the fears that had been imprisoning him for as long as he could recall.

"Lyra...," he started to say, his voice shaking as he took a shuddery breath. But before he could go any further, she stretched out, her hands to cover his face, holding him steady in the moment. "Just trust me," she said. "I won't turn away. I promise."

The sincerity in her eyes cut through his shield, and a spark of valor was kindled within his heart. With each pulsing beat, he felt an inclination to tell her everything, bare all the secrets that haunted him for centuries.

Under the stars, it seemed to fill the sky, whose expanse had been a witness to all the turmoil they both had undergone, lay the choice Alaric was on the precipice of making. Past shadows hissed warning in his ear, but the light in Lyra's eyes called out from them, urging him to follow the truth he had been denying for so long.

"I—" he started, his breath hitching into his throat.

The rustling of the leaves broke the spell, for a moment. Alaric's instincts told him to run, and he did, his heart racing in his chest as he cast a glance toward the darkness beyond the clearing.

"Back," he warned, the instinct to protect pushing up inside him as he placed himself between Lyra and whatever lurked in the darkness.

"What is it?" she asked, her face scrunched with confusion.

Before he could do anything, a figure came out of the trees—a dark silhouette, cloaked in shadows. Alaric felt the chill of recognition when the figure stepped into the moonlight to reveal a face he thought he'd long left behind.

"Alaric," it called, voice smooth and predatory, "we need to talk."

Lyra's heart pounded with fear as she clutched Alaric's arm and sensed the tension in him.

"Get away from her," Alaric hissed, instinctively stepping closer to Lyra, his protective nature flaring to life.

"Is that any way to greet an old friend?" the figure taunted, a smirk playing on their lips.

"Friend?" Alaric spat, the word dripping with disdain. "You're no friend of mine."

"Ah, but I have come with a proposition," the figure continued, eyes glinting with mischief. "You've been living in this little fantasy for too long, Alaric. It's time to face reality."

Lyra glanced between them, her heart pounding as she tried to comprehend the tension in the air. "Who are you?" she demanded, standing her ground beside Alaric.

"A relic from the past," he said, his eyes hard and calculating. "One who knows all the secrets Alaric has kept hidden."

"No," Alaric warned, his voice low and dangerous. "You're not going to ruin this."

"Ruin what?" he asked, playing dumb. "This little charade you've built with the girl who thinks she can save you? You think she can handle the truth?"

Lyra had anger surging up at the tone of the figure. "I can take truth, please," she said firmly; her voice was stable despite a fear churning in her belly. "Do you know something about Alaric?

He laughed, the deep dark sound making her shiver. "Oh, I know plenty. About his past, the lives he's taken, the darkness that lives within him. You really think you can love that away?"

"Enough," Alaric snarled, stepping forward, his rage churning under the surface. "You are not welcome here. Stay out of this.".

The figure raised an eyebrow, obviously enjoying the conflict. "But she's already in it, Alaric. You've dragged her into your world, whether you like it or not."

Lyra straightened beside Alaric, her heart pounding against her chest as she tried to make sense of the revelation. "What do you want?

"Simple," said the figure, whose voice dripped with malice. "I want to remind Alaric of who he really is. A monster hiding behind a mask and pretending to be something that he is not."

With that, the figure guided their attention back to Alaric's. Their eyes were gleaming challengingly. "You run from your past, but nothing ever lets you get that far. You think by hiding in the woods and this girl you can manage to get away from that? You think she saves you?

Alaric's rage flew forward, but then he glanced over at Lyra. And there was the iron look in her face. She stood beside him, and on her features was etched a mix of fear and anger. He couldn't let the words this figure was speaking get into her head about him.

"You don't know anything about her," Alaric said, savage. "You think you can intimidate me with threats? You are wrong.".

The figure laughed, a cruel sound that echoed through the clearing. "You can try to protect her, but it won't change who you are. She'll find out, eventually. They always do."

Alaric stepped closer to Lyra, his heart pounding. "I won't let you hurt her. You have no power here.".

The figure's smile grew even as a glint of mischief danced in his eyes. "We'll see about that. Shadows have a way of creep-ing back into the light, Alaric. You can't hide for much longer."

He had time for one final glimpse in her direction before turning again and disappearing back into darkness. The air settled immediately into an oppressive silence once he was gone.

Tense, heart pounding inside his chest, Alaric turned to face Lyra. "Are you okay?

She nodded, her calm demeanor betraying by the uncertainty in her eyes. "What just happened?"

He took a deep breath and tried to steady the racing of his heart. "That was someone from my past. Someone who knows the truth."

"About you?" she asked, terror creeping into her voice.

"Yes," he admitted, the weight of the revelation settling heavily between them. "And they're right about one thing—I can't hide from my past forever."

Lyra stepped closer, her eyes searching his. "But you can choose how to face it. You don't have to do it alone."

He stretched out his hand to take hers and felt the warmth of her touch ground him in the present. "I'm scared of what that truth could do to us," he said.

"Then let me in," she said, softly, her voice steady and unshaking. "Let me help you fight it."

In the cracks of her eyes, she showed a vulnerability that poked a hole in his armor. He felt driven to push forward and battle the demons looming over their heads. At that very moment, he realized that he couldn't keep running from it all.

"Alright," he said, a simple word left between them. He held the promise of doing it to his fragile attention, and thus he said: "I'll try".

The twinkling of the stars above him seemed to lift some of the weight from his fears. For the first time, he had a reason to confront the darkness he had always avoided, and that was Lyra.

Together, they would face whatever came next.

CHAPTER FIVE

VEIL OF DARKNESS

Their meetings continued but Lyra could not but feel that there was an undertone of sadness draped on Alaric's shoulder, weighing him down even on their lighter moments. There seemed to be a shadow attached to him, obscuring the shine in his eyes and muzzling the voice that should speak when she tried probing him too much about some matters. She tried, tenderly, to draw out more of his story, but he merely smiled in that absent way and turned the subject back on her. She could see the pain he tried to hide behind it, the fear edging his laughter, but she didn't know how to reach past it.

One night, as they trudged along a moonlit track further into the forest, Lyra decided to roll the dice. The air was sharp, full of the noises of nighttime animals. She proposed going along a track she'd never taken before, and that the unfamiliarity of the track might make him loosen up. Alaric agreed, though she saw how he seemed more awake, his movements careful and precise. As they walked, Lyra watched him closely, catching glimpses of how he seemed to blend seamlessly into the forest—how he moved with a grace that felt almost otherworldly.

Her curiosity burned brighter, but she kept her questions to herself. She, instead, shared a piece of her own story: of a loss she had faced years ago, when her closest friend had moved away, leaving her with an emptiness that had never fully healed. She spoke of how she had turned to the stars for comfort, how they had become a constant in a world that felt increasingly uncertain. Alaric listened quietly, his expression softening as she spoke. He could see pain behind words, the way she sought solace in the same sky that now connects them both.

Alaric felt a need to give her some piece of his story in return, inform her that he knew very well what it meant to lose someone, but no words came out of his mouth. He was afraid of once he started, he couldn't stop, that he would say too much. So instead, he reached out, a movement so slight she almost missed it, and laid a hand over hers. It was a simple touch, but it carried a depth of emotion he couldn't voice. Lyra squeezed his hand in return, offering him a small, sad smile. In that moment, the darkness between them seemed a mite less terrifying.

Their walk path was slim, the path bordered on both sides by tall trees that whispered secrets in the wind. As they walked on the woods, darkness came around them, building an unearthly atmosphere full of enchantment. The leaves gave some moonlight to fall into the ground, giving intricate designs as well as light through the road ahead. It filled Lyra with all the fresh air and with the earthy smell from breathing in the forest atmosphere, for which she would feel invigorated seeing the beauty around her.

But as they walked, Lyra saw how Alaric's expression changed. His eyes grew far away, and she could see the tension coiling in his shoulders. "Is everything okay?" she asked, her voice breaking the stillness.

He hesitated, then nodded, though the flicker of doubt in his eyes betrayed him. "Just... memories," he finally admitted, his voice low and hesitant. "This place feels different, more alive somehow. It brings things back."

It made Lyra's heart ache from the weight of his words. She wanted to know what tormented him; she wanted to help guide him through the pain that seemed only a hairline distance away. "You don't have to talk about it if you don't want to, but I'm here for you," she said softly.

Taking a deep breath, Alaric prepared himself for the swell of emotions that would surely drown him. "It's just..." He hesitated, seeking the perfect words. "There are pieces of me I've tried to forget. Shadows clinging to my mind, memories not willing to be free."

"Then let me carry them with you," Lyra said softly and warmly. "You need not carry it by yourself."

Alaric did not speak for a moment, torn between his need to open up to her and his instinct to shield her from his truth. He did not want to sully the light she brought to his life with his darkness. But when he looked at her sincere eyes, the walls of his heart began to crack. Maybe it was time to let someone in.

"I have made decisions that haunt me," he started slowly, his voice little more than a whisper. "Things I cannot alter, people I have lost. I have seen darkness, Lyra—darkness that stains the soul." His fingers felt hers tighten around him, urging him to say more. "I don't want to frighten you away. I've always thought it better to leave my past buried, but now. I find I cannot shake the feeling it is catching up to me."

Lyra's heart was racing. She felt a rush of empathy within her. "You are not defined by your past, Alaric. We all have shadows-we just have to learn how to face them."

He looked at her with his eyes, seeing conviction in her eyes. "I wish it were that simple. The things I've done. They are not easily forgotten."

"What have you done?" she asked softly, her curiosity tempered by concern.

He struggled hard, unable to swallow the truth that was spilling out. "I hurt people—innocent ones. It was many years ago, but that stain has stayed with me to this day. Like an inescapable scar.

Lyra felt a shiver run down her spine. She couldn't let him dictate what she should or shouldn't feel. "We all make mistakes. What matters is how we choose to move forward from them."

"But what if I can't move forward?" Alaric answered, despair weighing down the words of his voice. "What if I'm destined to be consumed by the darkness I've created?"

Then let's fight it together, she said firmly, her grip around his hand tightening. "You're not going through this alone, Alaric. I'm here, and I want to help you find light again."

He looked into her eyes. For a moment, it felt as though she had something powerful inside of her-strong enough to lead him past the fog of his life before. "Really you mean that?

Of course, Lyra replied, her voice unwavering. "You've shown me so much of yourself, and I care about you deeply. I want to understand your struggles so we can face them head-on.".

Alaric's heart swelled with a mix of thankfulness and fear. He wanted to believe her, to trust that she could take the truth he had held inside for so long. But doubt lingers in the back of his mind whispering that he was undeserving of her kindness.

Promise me you won't run away," he whispered, baring his vulnerability. "When I reveal the worst parts of myself, promise you won't see me as a monster."

"I promise," Lyra replied with absolute sincerity, her eyes sparkling. "I'm not afraid of you. I see the good in you, Alaric. Let's uncover the darkness together, one step at a time.".

When Alaric heard her words, he drew a deep breath into his lungs and steeled himself to bear the weight of truth he was about to reveal. "Long ago, I was lost—lost in a world of shadows. I became something I never wanted to be. I thought I could escape the darkness by embracing it, but it only pulled me deeper into a void.".

What do you mean? Lyra pressed lightly against him, her heart galloping as she experienced the power of his feeling.

"There was a time when I belonged to something horrible, something that fed on blood and terror. I thought that nothing could touch me, that my power would not cause any harm. But then I learned that everything is paid for," he revealed with a deep sigh. "I was blinded by ambition, and the main goal was to prove my self-worth. And in the process, I wronged people who did not deserve it.".

Lyra felt her heart tear at his words, racing to the countless implications that rose from within his past. "What happened?" she asked soft and gentle in case the flow of memories was still interrupted.

Eventually, I saw the destruction my deeds were causing. I walked away from the coven, but the guilt followed me around forever. It's taken years to avoid living through what I've lived through, to forget things," he said, with pain written on his eyes, telling about his life of remembrance. "And yet, it lingers and slowly makes its way into my life again.

Speaking, Lyra felt the mixture of fear and compassion that washed over him. She stretched out and wrapped her arms around him in a hug, enveloping him with a comfort that was deep. "You're not that man anymore, Alaric," she whispered. "You've changed. You're here now, at this moment, trying to do better. That is what matters.".

Holding her close, he felt his body warm from the feeling of her; the world did not seem to matter if he could hold onto a ray of hope that was hers. "But how will I know I won't backslide into the darkness? How can I be a man worthy of you?"

Lyra took a step back, looking for his eyes. "You already are that man," she said sharply, her voice unbroken. "You're fighting against your past, not letting it define who you are today. You're brave, Alaric. It takes a lot of courage to confront the shadows."

"But what if I can't defeat them?" he whispered, the doubt creeping back into his voice. "What if they consume me whole?

"Then we will face it together," she repeated, her conviction resolute. "I stand by your side, whatever it may be."

Her words settle into his chest, fragile but growing
hope. "I don't want to lose you."

He is raw and exposed; his vulnerability.

"You will not," she promised as she leaned closer. "Together we can find the way through this darkness.

Standing together, in the whispering silence of the forest, Alaric felt as if something had changed inside of him. He had been running for so long; maybe it was time to stand and face the shadows. With Lyra by his side, he finally found something to fight for.

The moon hung over them very high, shining its pale light over the clearing: a sign of the brightness that lives even in darkest night. Alaric looked down into Lyra's dark eyes, and something stirred within him - a fire that was more spark than flame, yet enough for him to step forward again.

Let's take this step together, he said, now his voice stronger. "I'll tell you more of my past, and we can figure out how to move on from here. But you have to promise me one thing."

"Anything," Lyra said, her heart racing with anticipation.

"Promise me you'll remind me of the light, even when I feel lost in the shadows.".

"I promise," she replied her voice steady as she repeated it. "We will find our own way.

At this moment, hands intertwined and hearts opened, Alaric felt the walls around his heart begin to crumble. The darkness was still present, but for the very first time in a long while, the spark of hope glimmered on-the-edge to regain strength enough to illuminate portions of the dark night ahead together.

CHAPTER SIX

FATE INTERVENED

That night, the accident just happened. Lyra had been urging a walk up one of the steeper trails-a trail that wound perilously near the edge of a ravine. The moonlight cast eerie shadows across the ground, turning the familiar woods into a landscape of silver and black. Alaric stayed close to her side, his senses on high alert, but he couldn't shake the unease that crept up his spine. The forest felt alive; every rustle and whisper heightened his awareness, making him acutely conscious of the danger they were wandering into.

As they walked closer to the ravine, a gust of cool wind swept over the trees, sending Lyra shivering down to her bones. She filled her lungs with air, desperately trying to rid herself of the ominous feeling that lay in the air. "I love how quiet it is out here," she said, smiling at Alaric, though it didn't quite reach her eyes. "It's as if the forest were holding its breath.".

Alaric nodded, his mind still racing with apprehension. "It can be peaceful, but it's important to be careful," he said, trying to mask his tension. "Some paths aren't as stable as they seem."

Just as he finished speaking, Lyra's foot slipped on a patch of loose soil. She let out a startled cry as she tumbled forward, her arms flailing for balance. The next instant, Alaric moved, his body reacting before his mind could catch up. He lunged forward with a speed that defied explanation, grabbing her arm and pulling her back from the edge. His grip was strong-too strong-and he lifted her effortlessly back onto solid ground. For a moment, they stood frozen, Lyra clutching his arm, her heart racing from the near fall.

Alaric...\" she panted, her eyes wide with shock. "That was... that was so fast." When she finally had caught her breath, she looked up at him, confusion mixed with the gratitude in her eyes. "How... how did you move so fast?

Alaric's mind ran wild for an explanation, his heart pounding in his chest. He tried to brush it off with a shrug and a forced smile. "Adrenaline, I guess," he said, but he could see the doubt in her expression, the way her eyes searched his face for answers. The truth hung heavily between them, a secret he was terrified to share.

Lyra did not press the matter, but the questions lingered between them. She watched him closely as they walked back to the clearing, noticing the tension in his posture, the way his jaw clenched with each step. "Are you okay?" she asked softly. "You seem... different. Is something bothering you?

Alaric swallowed hard, his mind churning a maelstrom of thoughts he hardly knew how to express. He muttered something under his breath, "I'm fine. Just.thinking," his voice sounding detached. He was afraid if he let himself say so much as a word, his entire world would pour forth.

They walked on in silence, the tension building between them. The moon was low in the sky; it had fallen toward the horizon, casting its silver glow down upon the earth, but Alaric felt the darkness still surrounding him. He had let her get far too close, and the final act that had saved her- from being killed by the Killer-also revealed to her the truth of his life: that the strength and speed were not adrenaline-just dark forces that accounted for it.

As they neared the meadow, Alaric's anxiety was growing in his chest; he could feel Lyra's inquisitiveness weighing against the surface of her mind-questions bubbling beneath her façade. She wanted to know him, and for that, he feared even more than anything. Maybe she would find out everything about him, discover just what he was: alive or dead? Would she have a chance to escape out of fear, or love him as he is in her heart?

When they came into the clearing, Lyra stopped, her face turning to him. "Alaric, please. I can see you are not being truthful with me. If there's something wrong, you have to tell me."

Her sincerity really pulled at his heart, but he hesitated and struggled with the fear that tormented him. "It's just..." he began, faltering over how to speak of the darkness inside him. "I don't want to drive you away."

"Scare me?" she repeated, furrowing her brow in puzzlement. "You could never scare me. But if you don't let me in, how can we move forward?"

Alaric felt his heart grow tight with the walls about it, like she were pressing down upon him by her gaze alone. He wanted to be honest; he longed to share this burden he had been carrying all these years. Yet a part of him was deathly afraid of what this might mean for them.

But just then, a low growl echoed through the trees, cutting through all tension like a knife. Alaric's instincts kicked in and his body tensed as he turned toward the sound. "Stay behind me," he said sharply, his voice low and commanding.

"What was that?" Lyra asked, her eyes now wide with alarm.

Just stay close," he coaxed, stepping in front of her protectively. The growling grew louder, echoing in the night, a sound filled with menace.

Out of the shadows, a dark figure emerged—a massive wolf, its fur gleaming in the moonlight, eyes glowing with an unsettling intensity. The creature paused at the edge of the clearing, its lips curled back to reveal sharp teeth. Alaric felt a rush of adrenaline, his instincts screaming at him to defend Lyra.

"Alaric!" she cried, fear creeping into her voice. "What's happening?"

Don't get up, he said slowly, his voice steady in his throat though his body had coiled tighter. The wolf took another step toward him. Its growl grew deeper, and he felt the air crackling with danger.

"Alaric, I do not want you to——

He interjected, feeling this primal energy surge within him-the part of him that had long been dormant. The wolf lunged forward and Alaric sprang to action, moving at a speed that was both exhilarating and terrifying.

He stepped aside, grabbed the nearest branch and swung it out at the beast, pressing it back. The wolf snarled; Alaric was a man on one thing- he would protect Lyra to his dying breath. The beast circled him, watching for an opening, his eyes locked on Alaric with an intensity that made a shiver run down his spine.

"Run!" Alaric called out to Lyra. "Get away from this place!

But Lyra stood unmoving, frozen by her inability to move her eyes from the scenes unfolding around her. "No! I'm not leaving you!"

The wolf leapt at him again. Alaric barely parried it in time, his fight-or-flight response kicking him into a ferocity he would never have thought he owned. He felt himself almost invincible, powerful through the rush of adrenaline to his senses, fueling his movements. He fought with an energy he thought he didn't possess at all. But the heaviness of his fear always lingered.

The battle seemed endless, and the wolf was relentless in testing Alaric's defenses. Every movement was sharp, driven by an instinct that pulsed beneath his skin. But in the back of his mind, he knew he was tapping into something dark, something he had tried so hard to suppress.

In a final, desperate lunge, Alaric swung the branch with all his might and struck the wolf. It let out a pained howl and went crashing to the ground. For a moment, everything was frozen—the forest held its breath, the air thick with tension.

Lyra's voice cut through the silence, full of a mix of fear and awe. "Alaric, are you okay?

He turned toward her, his chest rising and falling as he tried to catch his breath. "Get back!" he yelled, still on high alert, his instincts warning him that the danger wasn't over. The wolf was down but not defeated; it was merely regrouping, its eyes flashing with fury as it prepared to attack again.

When Alaric stood up, power streamed through him. For one moment, he was no longer quite himself. The darkness, which he'd kept under control all these years, grew so it began to blur the lines between the man and himself. He could feel this primal energy calling him to let out the beast within himself. But for Lyra standing there, shaking in terror but not stepping back, he fought it.

"Lyra!" he shouted, desperation creeping into his voice. "Get out of here! You have to get out!"

"I'm not going anywhere without you!" she shouted, stepping forward, without any regard for her danger.

"Damn it, Lyra!" he thundered, his heart running away with him as the wolf prepared to launch at him again. "You do not know what you're dealing with!"

But before he could utter another word, the wolf lunged at him again, and on impulse, Alaric ran toward it. He could have sworn he had more composure than this when, in a ferocity that he didn't think was in him, he dashed forward to intercept it. The world around them blurs into motion and sound as they collide.

Time stretched and warped, and for one instant, Alaric felt invincible. He was something more than man. Alaric fought the wolf with an intensity of a primal force springing because he wanted to save Lyra at whatever cost.

It felt endless, a survival dance with the creature, pushing back against its strength with all his willpower. And with every passing moment, he could feel himself slipping, darkness clawing its way free inside him. He struggled to contain it, keep it from overpowering the human in him, but it was a battle he was far from certain he'd win.

Just when it seemed that the wolf had it in its favor,

Alaric drew every last bit of strength into himself and pushed the creature back, so it was stumbling backward. Breathless, he wheeled about to see that Lyra still stood there, fear and worry written all over her face.

"Back!" he yelled once again, but the wolf charged them again.

This time, Alaric felt a shift inside his being; a power ran through him like a fire which lit within. He should protect her; he needs to tame the darkness that ate away at him. Wailing with a deafening roar, he charged towards her as man and beast was lost to his primal force tearing at his soul.

Alaric leaped at the wolf, straddling its back firmly and grapping for position. The animal thrashed under him with a menacing growl but Alaric had none of this mercy in him. This was an energy surging around him; for the very first time he felt what he did now. End.

With one last, final push of desperate energy, he tackled the wolf down to the earth and pinned it, where it let out an enraged howl at his strength as Alaric clamped down upon the wolf, and all the dark power inside of him refused to break loose as he channelled all of that into a singular will, keep Lyra safe no matter what.

With one final blow of strength, Alaric pushed the wolf away and sent it flying into a nearby tree. The creature lay there dazed and defeated, his eyes snapping with anger but he was not in the mood for fighting.

Panting and trembling, Alaric turned to face Lyra who stood wide-eyed and breathless taking all of it in before him. "Alaric..." she started, and he could see the fear in her eyes.

"Lyra," he said, his voice shaking. "Are you all right?"

"I'm fine," she replied, though her expression spoke of concern and confusion. "But what just happened? How did you do that?"

He wanted to open his mouth, wanted to explain himself; yet, the burden of this secret weighed down upon him, like a thick woolen cloak. He said too much already. "I... I do not know," he forced to his lips. "I simply needed to protect you.".

Her eyes searched his, trying to read the truth behind his words. "Alaric, you can't just brush this off. That wasn't normal. What are you hiding from me?"

He could feel the walls around his heart hardening again, the darkness creeping back in as he fought to keep himself together. "It doesn't matter," he said, his voice low and urgent. "What matters is that you're safe."

"Safe?" she repeated, incredulous. "How can I feel safe when I don't even know what you are?"

Alaric closed his eyes, fighting the turmoil within him. "You don't want to know," he whispered, his heart heavy. "If you knew the truth, you might not feel safe at all."

She took one more step closer, her voice steady and firm. "I want to understand, Alaric," she said. "I want to know you—the real you. We can't face this together if you keep shutting me out.".

He shook his head and couldn't help but avert his face. For him, these shadows hiding within him appeared too daunting, a door he could not open from his end. "I am not who you think me to be," he said to her with bitter words from his tongue.

The silence between them was deafening; the unsaid words were the unspoken fears, as Alaric sensed a distance developing between them. The thin connection built would be under the heavy burden of his secrets, like a tiny thread waiting to snap in the wind.

"Perhaps you are correct," Lyra said, finally speaking softly but surely. "Perhaps I know nothing about you. I want to know. I want to stay here with you, no matter how hard it might be.

Her honesty was like piercing darkness, filling him with a small glimmer of hope. "I do not want to drag you into my world," he confessed, letting spill the vulnerability he'd held deep inside him since finally locking eyes with her. "It's not safe for you. I do not want to hurt you.".

"You already saved me tonight," she said, stepping forward, determination shining in her eyes. "Whatever you are, I can face it. I just need you to trust me."

His heart ached at her words, but the shadows still loomed large. "Trust is hard for me," he admitted, his voice barely above a whisper. "I've spent so long pushing everyone away, building these walls...

Then let me help you tear them down," she said with eyes fierce and unyielding. "You're not going to face this on your own. You've proven there's light in the darkness, and I believe in you. Please let me in.".

For the first time in years, the weight of his secrets was lifting and the darkness receding. Taking a deep breath, Alaric searched her eyes for the strength she had offered, the warmth of her presence cutting through coldness that had consumed him for so long.

"I don't know if I can," he admitted, letting vulnerability spill out like confession. "But I will try. For you."

She smiled softly, relief palpable in her face. "That's all I ask."

They stood there together in the clearing, moon above and casting its gentle light down upon them, and Alaric felt a peace settle into his chest, a peace that would dispel the shadows that waited, just beneath the surface, but he was prepared to face them-together with Lyra by his side.

And in that moment, while the night's echoes whispered on, he was braver to believe perhaps, just perhaps, that a way through the darkness existed and waited to be found.

CHAPTER SEVEN

BETWEEN TWO WORLDS

The nights that followed the night of their close encounter with the wolf did not allow Alaric to forget the feeling that everything had changed. The air between him and Lyra crackled with tension, a silent battle fought in glances and half-formed thoughts. The weight of his secret pressed down on him, each unspoken word forming a barrier that felt more insurmountable with each passing moment. He knew he was at a crossroads—he could either continue to hide the truth that twisted within him like a thorn or risk everything by revealing who he truly was. But the thought of losing her, of seeing the warmth in her eyes replaced by fear, kept him silent.

The nights were quieter now, the forest around them seemingly more aware of their turmoil. They sat sometimes in the clearing where they'd first met, under a canopy of twinkling stars that seemed like far-off promises, but even the stars' beauty could not stand against the weight of the unspoken truth in the air. Alaric stood there and looked upon Lyra as she looked up at the constellations above her, her face moonlit, and his was an aching sense of longing coupled with dread. Every time he made eye contact with her, he wanted to spill everything that he had kept inside him, but the fear of being pulled away from the truth held him back.

One evening, when they sat together on a blanket strewn across the grass, the silence between them grew palpable. And Lyra turned to him, starlight shining softly on her face, and Alaric could see the determination shining in her eyes. "Alaric, I need to know...what really happened that night?" she asked, her voice gentle yet firm, and it cut through the heavy silence like a knife.

He could feel his heart racing with her question, but the truth waited at the tip of his mind and yearned to be released. He looked away, feeling himself weighed down by her gaze alone, as if it might penetrate to the most innermost recesses of his soul, where he'd have to give up the act and allow the monster he feared he was. He opened his mouth, and the words on the tongue of his mind, but fear clamped around his throat like a vice.

Instead, he talked about burdens he bore for years: mistakes he couldn't remove from his skin and a past that simply would not leave him alone. "I have always felt different, Lyra," he murmured, his voice cracked by shivering. "Ever since I was small, I knew there was something. wrong with me. Hard to put words on. My family could not understand it either. They said I was a freak.".

He spoke of disjointed memories of growing up, of the thrill of moonlit nights while others played beneath the sun, of running through the woods alone while other children laughed and played. He painted a picture of loneliness, the isolation that wrapped around him like a shroud, but he held back the truth that lay deeper within.

Lyra listened carefully, her face softening into expressions of empathy, as starlight reflected in her eyes. Yet, as he spoke, he could sense she felt his restraint, that he still held back his most important pieces. Through sharing his story, he sensed her presence urging him open up, to unveil the darkness that lurked at the edges of his soul. She reached out, her fingers brushing against his arm, a gesture that sent warmth flooding through him. "Please, Alaric, I need you to continue."

Just as he was about to speak—just as he was on the verge of revealing the secret that had haunted him—fear surged through him. He recalled all the times he had been too careless, how people would turn to look at him once they knew the truth, that horror and rejection written on their faces. He could not forget those times as the flame of bravery he had ignited flickered in his mind. He could not bear to look at Lyra with fear in her eyes. So he stepped back, retreated again into the silence that became his sanctuary. "I... I just want to protect you," he blurted out, though even to his own ear, the words felt vacant. He could see how her face would crumple at the disappointment there but did not have enough will to explain, lay himself bare in a way it would leave him defenseless.

She felt his turmoil, the pain unspoken in his words. Her brows knitted as she studied him, but though she didn't ask him anything more, her gaze said it all. "Alaric," she said softly, "whatever it is, I'm here for you. I promise that when you're ready to share, I'll be here to listen.".

The promise hung there, a gossamer thread weaving hope into the fragile tapestry of their fragile connection. Even so, however, he still felt that fear, an insistent shadow that wouldn't let him go. He wanted to believe one day he would be ready to let go and bare himself for her, but doubt ate at the edges of his resolve.

And so they sat together under the stars, two souls caught between worlds, bound by secrets and unspoken hope that one day, the truth would no longer stand between them.

Days ran into each other, one an uncomfortable duplicate of the other, spent crawling through stilted silences and half-hearted conversations. Lyra attempted to draw Alaric out with suggestions of walks, picnics, and stargazing but a tension hung over them like a storm cloud, waiting to break. Alaric felt the walls he'd built around himself closing in on him with every interaction reminding him of a truth he hadn't yet revealed.

One afternoon, wandering in the woods, Lyra's laughter seemed like music, sweet as she moved around gathering wildflowers, braiding them into a crown while talking excitedly about her dreams, about her future. "I want to travel the world," she declared, eyes sparkling with enthusiasm. "There's so much to see out there, Alaric. I want to experience everything.".

Inside, he felt the sting of sorrow as he listened to her words. He remained still in the world he'd created for himself, where shadows danced at the edge of his vision and light was nothing but a faraway memory. "You should," he said low, his voice barely audible. "You deserve to see the world and experience all its wonders.".

She stopped, turning towards him inquiringly. "What about you? What do you want?

He opened his mouth to respond, but truth choked him. He craved freedom from his own past, from the binding chains that kept him tied in fear. He wanted her life, wanted to savor the beauty of everything they could build together-how could he when the darkness loomed so large? Instead he said, "I don't know yet. Maybe I'm still figuring it all out."

Lyra furrowed her brow and could almost see the worry etched in her face. "You don't have to work everything out alone, okay? I'm here for it. Whatever it is, we can face it.

Her words hung in the air, a lifeline reaching out into the dark that had engulfed him, a lifeline flailing in the dark forlornly. He should believe her, reach to take her hand in such a tight grasp that with one pull he would carry her into the flicker of light just beyond reach. But the shadows darkened more than ever - a constant reminder of the hole between them.

Days turned into weeks, yet Alaric remained inside a circle of silence; every moment spent with Lyra was both a boon and a curse. She insisted on breaching his walls, though he admired this persistence, making him all the more afraid. He well knew that her patience wore thin; the glints of concern in her eyes increasingly became impossible to hide behind.

And there's a night, when they sat in their clearing under stars, that the weight of the moment came down upon Alaric like an oppressor. Lyra looked at him with a seriousness in her eyes, and he felt his heart racing. "I've been thinking," she said, her voice steady. "Perhaps we need to talk about the elephant in the room."

His breath caught in his throat as the reality of her words crashed over him like a wave. "What do you mean?"

"The truth," she said, her gaze unwavering. "Whatever it is you're hiding, it's time to share it. I can't keep wondering what's in your heart. You need to trust me, Alaric.".

And then the walls crumbled in around him, the desperation in her voice piercing through his carefully constructed defenses. "I can't," he whispered, his voice breaking under the strain of emotion. "You don't know what I'm carrying.".

"Then explain to me!" she pleaded, frustration creeping into her voice. "You are not the only one who matters here. I care about you, and I cannot bear to see you suffer in silence."

His eyes began to tear at the corners as her words hit him so hard. "I'm scared, Lyra," he admitted, his voice barely above a whisper. "I'm terrified of what you'll think of me when you find out. What if you're not ready for the truth?

"Then help me be ready," she said, her voice softening, reaching for his hand. "I don't want to be left in the dark anymore. If you keep holding me at arm's length, it'll only drive us apart."

Alaric looked at her, really looked, and in that moment,

His sight caught the unyielding powers in her eyes, such as the light pushing to pierce through the depths of his terror. Yet, it frightened him- he still knew he could no longer be a slave to what was dark within him; perhaps it was time he stepped into the light that would let her see for what he really was.

With a deep breath, he finally opened his mouth, letting out the words like an unsaid confession. "I am not just this lonely guy, Lyra. There is so much more. I am different in ways you can't even think of."

"How?" she asked, looking fascinated as her eyes widened wide with interest.

"I... I am not human," he stammered, the confession tasting strange on his tongue. "Not fully, at least. I have a lineage... a heritage that makes me what I am."

Lyra didn't say a word, her face going through different expressions as she digested his words. "What do you mean?"

"I come from a world that lives in the dark. It is a world of beasts that most people cannot believe exist." He stopped, contemplating the gravity of the situation. "I am part of the line of elder people—vampires."

The word lingered there, heavy and powerful. Lyra opened her mouth, her eyes widely spread, with incredulous lines carved across her face. "Vampires?"

His heart thumped as he met her gaze, nodding hard. "Yes, true. Part of my family history. I have darkness in me, Lyra, and I have fought my life to fight it off."

"Is that why you've been distant?" she whispered on a quiet voice.

"Yes," he said, the weight of his admission settling between them. "I did not want to drag you into my world, to show you all the darkness that I carry. I thought it would be safer for you if I kept you at arm's length."

"But I want to be close to you," she said softly, her voice full of conviction. "I want to understand all of you, even the parts that scare you. You don't have to face this alone."

Alaric searched her eyes for a glimmer of fear, horror he had expected but instead saw something else: curious and compassionate. "You don't know what you're asking," he cautioned, his voice shaking.

"Then explain it to me. Help me see your world," she demanded relentlessly. "I want to stand by your side, no matter what that might entail.".

Looking at her changed everything. It made fear's grip ease off for him, as if somehow, in his own body, the light flickering in her heart lit in his. He had been hidden in shadows far too long, and perhaps it was time to take a walk into the light. But maybe, just maybe with Lyra, he would discover a way to connect this world to his own after all.

He nodded slowly, taking a deep breath. "Okay," he said, the weight of his decision settling over him. "But you have to promise to stay with me, no matter how dark it gets."

"I promise," she said, her voice steady and reassuring.

And as they sat together in the clearing, above them shining brightly the stars, Alaric could feel the first stirrings of hope—a frail thread weaving through the darkness, connecting their two worlds in ways he had never imagined possible. Together they would face the unknown and step bravely into the future that awaited them.

CHAPTER EIGHT

DISTANCE OF FEAR

The days became weeks, and the warmth that had once seemed to emanate from Alaric's presence started to fade like dying embers. He had never wanted this to happen; he had never wanted to draw away from Lyra, the one person who had started to unravel the tightly wound layers of his heart. However, the risk his emotions for her were taking was becoming too obvious, weighing down on him with an insistent pressure. Alaric knew he had to choose between his emotions and her safety. Every time he felt the urge to reach out to her, to meet her in their secret clearing beneath the stars, he was met with a haunting dread that gripped his chest and held him captive.

In his heart, Alaric knew that the only way to save her from the shadows that crept into his past was to keep away. The longer he stayed with her, the more danger he posed of exposing her to the dangers of his world: his coven, the darkness of his existence, and the eternal threat that loomed over him like a specter. So he stopped showing up at the regular trysting places and sidled out of the clearing, as if it was an off-limits sanctuary. Whenever he caught sight of her out of the corner of his eye, hovering at the edge of the woods, it hurt him to the point of tears, but he left, telling himself that that was for the best.

The more he stayed away, the more hollow his insides felt, hollow like a shell of man, the person he had once been. His days were marked by an unsightly routine: school, library, and home—at every moment spent not at Lyra's side edged into his chest the ache. The laughter that had been so easy for her to find now seemed a long way away, and even the sun set when she wasn't there. He would pace at night in his little room, surrounded by shadows that reminded him of what he had done. It was too heavy to bear, yet he clung to it as the only lifeline he knew to keep Lyra safe.

Lyra left confused and hurt amidst the whirlwind. She had her heart torn between two opposing feelings. She became the mercy of a cold wind sweeping through her soul and made her naked and lost because of the sudden change in Alaric's personality. She could hardly recognize the boy who had shared her dreams under the stars and listened to her stories with such tender interest. Now, he was a ghost of himself: a distance, coldness, and evasiveness about him. Every time they bumped into each other in town or at school, Alaric's words were curt and brief, as if he were building a citadel around his heart, and she was standing outside with no way to break the walls.

She was furious and frustrated, which brewed inside her like a burning fire that compelled her to look for answers. "What did happen to you?" she wanted to shout. She caught up with him outside class, her voice cracking with urgency. "Alaric, please, talk to me! I don't understand why you're acting this way." But he would just shrug her off, his eyes avoiding hers, unwilling to let her see the turmoil that churned inside him.

And with each meeting, a part of Lyra dissolves into nothingness, absorbed by the shadows that seem to consume Alaric.

"Why are you shutting me out?" she implored one afternoon, cornering him against the lockers. The hallway buzzed with students rushing to their next classes, but to Lyra, the world had fallen silent, leaving just the two of them in a bubble of strained emotion. "I can't stand watching you push me away!"

"I'm not sending you away," he said gruffly, his voice without conviction. He raked a hand through his hair, frustration clear in his posture. "I just. need some space."

"Space? You think that's what I need? You think that's what will make this better?" She crossed her arms, her heart racing with anger and despair. "You're making it worse, Alaric! I can't help you if you won't let me in."

For a moment, she glimpsed a flicker of something almost like fear in his eyes, and he showed her the vulnerability beneath the façade. He shut down, retreating behind walls he had built. "You don't understand," he muttered, his eyes slumping to the floor. "You have no idea what I'm dealing with."

No, I don't!" she exclaimed. "But I want to!" Her voice rose on a crescendo. "You're my best friend, Alaric! I cannot simply stand by and watch you suffer alone!" She begged on her knees, pleading for him to please talk to her. But the moment had come and gone; he turned from her. And in that instant, she lost a piece of herself. That night, she lay in bed, staring at the ceiling as her heart felt heavy with worry. She couldn't shake off the feeling that something dark loomed over him, a shadow threatening to consume him whole.

She thought of the stories she read, the ones that spoke of ancient curses and hidden dangers, and wondered if Alaric was caught in a web of his own making. Alaric kept a safe distance, observing Lyra; his heart writhing in torture. He felt an unbearable urge to narrow the gap he had placed between them and bring her closer. He would lean forward to whisper all about the real depth of emotions within his chest, only to turn away and flee because of the horror-filled ghost haunting him every now and then - a threat of perils that lingered about him. In his head, war reigned against the thoughts themselves. He tried to talk himself into believing it was for the best—that this distance would keep her safe.

But during the still quiet moments, when the stars blinked down at him like a million tiny eyes, he felt the hollowness of his decision. So now the lonely Alaric comes alone to sit by chance at sundown on a wooden park bench, and it isn't until he looked toward the stars that those many constellations stared upon his soul. This constant reminder of what they are no longer was nothing as it compared to those silhouettes of trees by Lyra's chuckling warmth and light about it. It was something too brutal: the trade had already been made for sure with all that safety now standing there like a poor choice he couldn't claim against it. He then saw her afar, her shape outlined against the fading light. She looked lost, a solitary flower in a field of shadows.

He yearned to reach out to her, to call out her name, but the fear of her seeing the monster that he might become made him hold his tongue.

Then for a few more days, he became even more evasive from her. He cancelled their plans with excuses that he was ill or needed to study. All the reasons were a twist of knives in his abdomen, yet he found reasons to excuse it. He buried himself with schoolwork; he flooded his time with assignments and textbooks in hope that, by doing this, the pain could dull down with busy hours. But all those passing minutes only heaved the weight of the guilt on him as if stuck.

Lyra refused to let this stop her. She felt the battle within him, the shadows dancing in the back of his eyes. Every time he turned his head away, she saw an inner fire blaze to a more fierce determination. Alaric was fighting for a battle she could not see, and she couldn't stand idly by. With every ounce of courage she could muster up inside herself, she had to reach him, to possibly confront the darkness swallowing him whole.

The next time she saw him in school, she steeled herself and approached him at lunch. "We need to talk," she said sternly, her heart racing. Alaric sat at a table with some classmates, but his eyes jerked away from hers as if he were in the middle of doing something wrong.

I am busy," he replied shortly, but Lyra wouldn't let him off the hook so easily.

"No, you're not. You have been avoiding me for weeks. If you cannot tell me what's wrong, then I'll have to figure it out myself," she insisted, her voice unwavering.

"Lyra, please, just drop it," he said, frustration lacing his tone. "I am fine. Just need some space.".

Fine? You're not fine! This isn't you! You're shutting everyone out, and I won't let you shut me out either!" Her words were yelled out into the bustling cafeteria, echoing out for other students nearby to hear. Alaric's eyes narrowed, and for a second, she was convinced he was going to pop.

"Because I love you!" The words slid out before she could close her mouth, the truth of her emotions tumbling over them like a tide. The table fell silent, with a few heads turning toward her in shock.

Alaric's face went through a transformation, as if surprise flickered across his eyes but was immediately doused in a guarded look. "You don't know what you're saying," he told her, his voice so low it almost quivered.

"I know what I'm saying, Alaric!" she insisted, her heart racing. "I don't care about your past or your secrets. I care about you! You're pushing me away, and I don't understand why!"

He looked away, his jaw tightening as if he were fighting a battle within himself. "You don't understand, Lyra. I'm not safe. My life isn't what you think it is."

Then tell me! I can't help you if you won't let me in, she pleaded, her voice softer now, the urgency replaced by a heartfelt desperation.

Alaric's resolve faltered for just a moment, and she could see the cracks in his facade. But then he shook his head, the walls rising again. "I can't," he said, voice heavy with the weight of his decision.

"You don't want to know the truth."

"Try me," she dared, her heart beating rapidly. "You've been there for me. Now let me be there for you."

But he merely rose, scraping the chair loudly on the floor. "I just can't do this now," he murmured, then walked away from the table, and out of her life with her confession echoing in between.

Lyra watched him walk away, frustration churning in her chest, but beneath it lay a deeper sense of fear. The farther he went, the closer danger clung to him; not just to Alaric, but to herself. She did not know what he was hiding, but she could feel its weight, an imminently threatening presence that seemed just out of reach.

That evening, going home under the shroud of dusk, determination washed over her. If Alaric wouldn't go to her, then perhaps she would have to be the one to go to him. She had to figure out a way to reach beneath the carefully constructed walls-the boy she knew lay trapped there.

As darkness crept over the small town, Lyra leaned against the woods, observing into the dark. Whatever had passed in that now seemingly world-distant clearing seemed so impossible that she'd give up everything to find her man again. She did one step forward into the woods and another, pacing forward without wavering about her footfall.

"Alaric!" she raised her voice as it spread across the woods. "I know you are here!

Silence said nothing, but approached, her heart hammering loudly in her breast; and every step she went the more this air of oppression grew heavy as with wood itself holding its very breath. "Please tell me just something!" she pored once more, desperation uniting with fear.

Moments later, she heard rustling in the underbrush, and Alaric stepped into view, his face a mix of surprise and annoyance. "What are you doing here?" he demanded, his voice edged with tension.

"I came to find you," she said, trying to keep her voice steady. "You can't keep running away from this.".

"I told you to stay away!" he snapped, but something in his tone softened, easing the tension in his body as he regarded her.

"Why? Because you're afraid? Because of what you're hiding? Whatever it is, you're stronger than this fear," she pressed, stepping closer. "You can't shut me out, Alaric. Not anymore."

He looked torn, his eyes manufacturing a storm as he fought with her words. "You don't understand, Lyra. My life is dangerous. It is not just me who is in danger, it is you too. You will only bring harm to yourself by pursuing this.".

And let me decide that for myself! I want to stand by you, no matter what," she declared, her voice steady. "You're not alone in this, Alaric. You never were.".

A minute silence hung between them like something crackling in the air, heavy with what went unspoken and was forced down. Alaric's mask broke apart; he ran a frustrated hand through his hair and drew a deep breath with those words etched in features of frustration. "I can't let you get hurt because of me. You deserve a normal life, one without darkness surrounding me."

"But I don't want normal!" she shot back, her frustration boiling over. "I want you! You're the one who makes me feel alive! If you push me away, it'll kill me faster than anything else!"

Alaric's expression softened, and she could see the war raging within him. "Lyra..." he began, his voice faltering.

No more excuses! she shouted, her heart racing with another step forward that took her closer to him. I do not fear the darkness, Alaric. I fear losing you.

His eyes probed hers, and for the first time she saw something like a glimmer of hope mixed with the shadows. You don't know what you're asking for, he said in a voice barely above a whisper.

"Then show me," she urged, her breathing steady. "Show me everything."

And with that, under the unmoving stars, Alaric felt the threads of his past begin to snap loose. The weight of his choice crushed down on him, but Lyra's set purpose flared bright like a torch in the night. Maybe, just maybe, there was a way to confront the monsters inside without losing her.

He took in a deep breath and nodded, the decision settling in his heart. "Okay," he said, the words filled with both trepidation and relief. "But you have to promise me one thing: if it gets too dark, if the shadows close in. you have to run. Promise me you'll run."

"I promise," she said, her voice even. And there they stood together in the clearing, with the stars shining brightly above them, and Alaric felt the first tentative flickers of hope: a fragile thread worked and woven through the shadows to connect their worlds in ways he had never dreamed possible. Together, they would face the unknown, and step into it, both holding hands.

CHAPTER NINE

CONFRONTATION UNDER THE STARS

It was a tense night, heavy with the weight of tension, when Lyra finally reached the clearing. A place she had once called home, and the stars were there in the sky, twinkling with an almost mocking brightness. They lit up the space that had held so many of their shared moments. She found Alaric standing at the edge, his silhouette stark against the night sky, and her heart ran with a mix of hope and fear.

"Alaric! " she exclaimed, her urgency tearing across the stillness of the night. He turned, brought awake by a jolt, as waking from a trance, but only for a heartbeat and not more than the fraction of a second till stillness lay silent, full of unvoiced words between them. "Why do you avoid me?" Lyra demanded imperatively, frustration bursting forth from her as she strode forward.

"I try to reach you, but you just... you just push me away.
What's going on?
"

Alaric's face steeled, a reflexive wall sliding into place. "Lyra, it is not what you think," he said, his voice clipped and distant. He could feel the walls closing in on him, the pressure of her gaze heavy with expectation. "You don't understand.".

Then tell me!" she fired back, frustration giving way to anger. "I don't know what I did to make you shut me out, but I deserve to know the truth!" Her heart was racing as she watched him struggle, his eyes flickering with emotions he refused to voice.

The air crackled with tension, and for one moment, it seemed the stars themselves were holding their breath, waiting for Alaric to say something.

He opened his mouth to protest, to deflect her questions, but something in him shifted. She pushed him to the edge, and her determination was a flame igniting the kindling of his own fears.

I saved you from falling, didn't I?" he finally replied, the words bursting forth in a heated rush. "But it's not just that. There's more to it than you realize, Lyra. I can't be the person you think I am.".

"Then tell me!" she said in a voice heavy with despair, desperation creeping in. "Tell me what's going on! I see how you look at me. I see the way you talk to me. You care, Alaric, but you're scared to death of showing it. Why?"

The dam inside Alaric burst open; his emotions poured out, flowing through a broken levee like water. His breath stuck in his throat as he fought the compulsion to reveal everything. He opened his mouth to say something, but just then, fear clutched him. What if she rejects me? What if she turns away in horror from the truth I've kept inside me for centuries?

Lyra, I. He paused, hesitant to speak between the need for silence and the threat of vulnerability. She was already chipping away at the walls he erected to guard his heart, and now she was being shown the unfamiliar threat of powerlessness.

Argument flared between them both, each seeking to speak over the other. The urgency in Lyra's tone was at odds with Alaric's defiance, the air charged with words left unsaid. She could sense the desperation of the instant, how their worlds crashed into each other in the dance of light and darkness. In this heated dialogue, Alaric found himself on the edge of revelation as truth clawed its way to the surface.

Finally, at the height of his passion, Alaric let a peek of his true self slither through. "Don't hurt me!" he screamed, his voice laced with raw emotion. "You have no concept of what I am; the darkness that surrounds me." The vulnerability in his voice cut through the tension, and Lyra felt her heart skip a beat. Brought to the surface in his defiance was a pain deeper than she could have even imagined.

Then let me in!" she pleaded, her voice a little shaking. "I am not afraid of the darkness. You are not alone, Alaric. I care about you—just tell me what's going on!

For a moment, he looked as if he might collapse under the weight of her words. She saw a flicker of something in his eyes—fear, perhaps, or an ache that mirrored her own. But just as quickly, the shutters fell back into place, the protective mask reasserting itself.

"Lyra, I can't," he whispered quietly, his voice steady, though heavy with sorrow. "You don't know what you're asking. It's not just me this is about; it's what I am. I wouldn't take you to my world. I couldn't let you be a part of it."

Your world? You mean the world that you've hidden from me? she shot back, not letting him get away with dismissal. If you keep this up, you'll only push me further away! You think that's what's best for me? You're wrong!

Maybe it is!" he snapped, frustration welling up inside. "You think you can handle it, but you have no idea what it means to be with someone like me. You think it's all moonlight and stars, but there's darkness in my soul, and it's dangerous.

She echoed, heart racing. "Dangerous?" or just different? You have been there for me, Alaric. You shared with me, joy and pain. Why can't you trust me to do the same for you?

Alaric turned away, forcing himself not to show his frustration. Shadows seem to deepen around them, gulping a light that earlier made its presence so welcoming. He whispered, "I really don't want you exposed to my world. My life isn't worth living for.".

Between them, a heavy silence settled, full of unsaid emotions. Lyra felt the weight of his words settle around her like a shroud, and took a step closer. Her heart racing, she spoke softly, her voice unwavering. "You are worth the risk. You're worth everything to me," she said softly. "I love you, Alaric. I can't lose you.".

The confession was heavy in the air, and for a fleeting instant, it revealed the whole facade of Alaric. She saw everything: the battling going on inside him. Part of him wanted to claim her and part of him was terrified by what that would mean.

"Lyra," he said, his voice shaking, but the tension of the moment broke on the faint rustle of leaves that had burst up at the edge of their hiding place. Both of them remained silent, breath thumping in chest, a tall figure standing out from within the shadows. Alaric's eyes opened wide into full recognition, and he stepped forward, instinctively placing himself before Lyra to block his view.

"Alaric," the figure spoke, his voice dripping with disdain and authority. "I should have known I'd find you here, consorting with a mortal. You always were a fool."

Lyra's pulse leapt as she looked at the newcomer. The figure stepped into the moonlight, and a face emerged that was both familiar and unsettling. It was Seraphine, Alaric's coven leader, her presence predatory in a way that made Lyra's skin crawl.

"What are you doing here?" Alaric asked, his voice tense, with an urgency Lyra had never heard before. "This is none of your business.

Contrarily, it's very much my business," Seraphine countered with a sly curl of the lip. "You have secrets, Alaric and little does it seem to bode well for the involvement of your little play thing. I won't permit it."

"Hands off!" Alaric roared, moving between the girl and Seraphine. "This isn't some kind of game now. You don't control what happens in my life, Seraphine.".

"Oh, but I do," she said with heavy condescension. "You've forgotten your place haven't you? You think that you can escape the mess of your past but the past will always find a way to get you. And it will destroy the person who gets too close.

"Lyra is not a pawn in your games!" Alaric spat, anger burning him. "You don't get to decide who I care about or what I do with my life."

Seraphine's eyes flickered with amusement, her gaze shifting from Alaric to Lyra, taking in every detail. "And you, sweet mortal," she said, her voice dripping with false sweetness. "Do you truly believe you can save him? He's more than you could ever comprehend. Love is a dangerous illusion in our world.".

"I don't need you to tell me what I can or cannot understand," Lyra shot back, her anger rising like a flame. "I care for Alaric, and I will not let you bully him."

"He doesn't change what he is," Seraphine replied, her smile fading from her face. "You are playing a dangerous game, and you have no idea of the stakes. Leave now while you still can, or you will find yourself caught in the crossfire of a war you cannot possibly win."

She stood firm, heart thumping with the pressure of Seraphine's stare. She could feel the darkness around her: a living thing that was threatening to engulf everything it touched. But in this moment, her resolve solidified. "I'm not backing down," she said. "I'm not letting you take him from me."

Alaric turned to Lyra, pulled between the compulsion to defend her and the fear of what Seraphine

might do if he didn't keep himself guarded enough. "Lyra, please..." he started, but she shook her head, cutting him off.

"No more running, Alaric. We can face this together. I won't let her control your life."

Seraphine let out a laugh, her voice cold, cruel; it sent chills all through the air. "Together? Oh, a quaint notion, don't you think? Your love to withstand the storms that approach? I've seen empires crumble for that. Alaric, you're such a fool to believe your human attachment can save you from that fate that waits for you."

"Enough!" Alaric shouted, his anger surging him forward one step, blocking Lyra from Seraphine's view. "You get to decide my fate no more! I am finished with your threats and manipulations. This is my life, and I shall choose whom I stand by."

Her eyes narrowed, a flicker of rage igniting in the depths of them. "You will regret this, Alaric. You may have turned your back on your past, but your past hasn't turned its back on you. I will not allow you to throw it away so carelessly.".

A wave of her hand was all it took, shadows twisting around her like a living cloak, darkness pulsing with anger. "You think you can defy me? You'll find yourself alone, abandoned by your precious human. And when the darkness comes for you, you'll wish you'd taken heed of my warning.".

"Leave us!" Alaric shouted, his voice echoing through the clearing, resonating with a power he didn't fully understand. "You are no longer welcome here!"

Seraphine paused and changed her expression from a fiery anger to something almost humorous. "You think you can protect her?" she asked, leaning forward. "How the great knight is noble of you. But the thing is much more complicated than you can ever imagine. Remember this moment, Alaric. When shadows come to collect what belongs to them, you are going to be alone.".

With that, she turned and melted into the dark in an unsettlingly gracious move, leaving behind the atmosphere of foreboding to linger like a bad omen.

Lyra was paralysed for what felt like an eternity; the echo of Seraphine's words stuck inside her head. Her stomach began to knot itself as she turned to Alaric, whose face she could see was chiselled into a combination of determination and fear.

"What was that about?" she asked, her voice not quite steady.

Alaric rubbed a hand through his hair, clearly frustrated. "It's not that simple. She comes from a world I am trying to keep myself disconnected from. She's having a hard time letting go."

"But you stood your ground," Lyra asserted, her voice growing strong. "You did not step down to her level. She intimidated you. That should mean something.

It doesn't make me different, he countered, his voice heavy with the weight of confession. I am not some stargazer boy. There's blackness inside of me and it may just threaten to hurt you.

Then we should face it together, she said firmly, advancing nearer, requiring him to be clear on her side. She wouldn't let him exclude her anymore. She loves him, Alaric, and wouldn't stand down. He looked into her eyes and in that instant she saw the battle inside him. "I don't want to hurt you, Lyra. That's all I ever wanted. I can't let you get mixed up in this mess." "You have mixed it, Lyra," she breathed gently. "And I wouldn't change it for the world. Please, just let me in.". Alaric closed his eyes, holding his breath as he struggled with the whirlwind of emotion inside him.

He sensed the weight of her look, the love she thrust at him like a lifeline, pulling him back from the shadow that had always followed him.

"I don't know how to do this," he admitted, his voice cracking. "But if we're going to face this together, we need to know what we're dealing with."Lyra nodded, her heart pounding in her chest. "Then let's figure it out together. We'll start with the truth." They stood before it as two souls with nothing but sheer courage to connect the two into a battle face with anything that surrounded dark shroud ahead. As with all darkness surrounding their back and even above, as stars twinkle, they finally joined together what would eventually clash the strongest strength in holding out together for each the days yet to pass.

CHAPTER TEN

A Sanctuary's Echo

The forest was coming alive with the sounds of night as Alaric led Lyra deeper into the woods, his heart pounding with a mix of anticipation and fear. He could feel every step; each one felt monumental to him. The air hung heavy with the weight of their shared secret. The two walked side by side under the silver glow from the moonlight filtering down through the branches. The night was cool, the leaves above rustling from a gentle breeze, which was adding a layer of magic to the atmosphere.

Finally, they reached a secluded grove where the trees parted to reveal ancient stone ruins, covered in ivy and shadows. This took Lyra's breath away with a haunting beauty emerging from the darkness. It was as if time had forgotten this place, leaving it untouched and serene.

"This place... it once was a sanctuary for my race," Alaric said quietly, his voice little above a whisper. Moonlight plays on the worn stones as it casts an ethereal shadow to dance upon the ground. "It is centuries old. Centuries ago, it flourished as a sanctuary for people who sought shelter from the world."

She moved forward, her fingers tracing the moss-covered stones, and the history of the place began to seep into her soul. "It's beautiful," she whispered softly, her voice full of awe. She turned to him, curiosity igniting in her gaze. "What happened here?

Alaric took a deep breath of the air, memories flooding as he took in the state of the ruins. "We were a coven, united by loyalty and love. This was a place to be ourselves, without any fear of judgment. Yet, over time, fights began to break out among us. Our existence had become a secret burden. Many of us chose the shadows instead of risking our exposure.".

He paused, a flicker of pain crossing his face. "I used to be part of that world. But when the conflicts started getting violent, I lost everything. I had to leave. to survive.

As he spoke, a deep well of empathy over him washed over Lyra. The weight of his words settled heavily in the air between them. She laid her hand on his arm, bringing him back to the present. "You've borne so much pain," she said softly, her voice full of understanding. "I don't think I could bear it if I'd watched everything you did, especially with all that loss around you."

Alaric met her eyes, his vulnerability there unrestrained. "It was a burden I thought that I would bear for the rest of my days. It feels different here with you. For the first time, I could see just a glimmer of hope.

Lyra squeezed his arm lightly, her heart swelling with both love and sorrow. "You do not have to carry it alone anymore," she said calmly. "I am with you, Alaric, every step of the way. You are more than your past.".

Just at this point, as they were gazing into the ruins all round them, the atmosphere started to shift. A feel of peace enveloped their being, covering them as if in a protective veil. The tension that started with their earlier argument had begun to thaw away to be replaced by nascent trust. Lyra would feel the weight lift from Alaric's back as he let his thoughts open up to the consideration that maybe a future didn't have to be about the isolation.

"Would you like to know more about the coven?" he asked, his voice softer now, as if he were afraid to disturb the delicate tranquility surrounding them.

"I would love that," she replied, her eyes sparkling with interest.

Alaric stepped a move back. He brought his vision downwards to gaze at the intricacies carved on stone walls: "The coven was akin to some form of my family, after all. We bared our biggest concerns, greatest fears alongside our thoughts we did not want. In the night, with every full moon, there used to come here at full-moon nights that are allowed within this wild because of sky and as completely free beneath an uncloistered world of bonds formed for love or bond for trusting.

She could see it in her mind, a scene full of life and light. "What made you change?" she asked softly, for she knew there was more to the story.

"The world outside grew restless," he replied, a shadow passing over his features. "Humans began to hunt us, fearing what they didn't understand. Our sanctuary became a target, and those of us who remained had to choose between fighting for our home or fleeing to survive."

"Did you fight?" she asked, her heart racing at the thought of him in battle.

Alaric nodded, but his face darkened. "We fought hard, but it was never enough. The rifts in our coven grew, fueled by fear and loss. In the end, I lost my closest friends, those I considered family. The cost was too high, and I chose to leave rather than watch more die."

Her heart felt a pang of pain as she thought of the pains he had to endure, but she could only guess how it must have been like. "I don't know how that must feel," she said softly and reached for his hand. "But you are no longer that person. You're here now, and you can start anew."

Do you really believe that?" he asked, looking at her with a mixture of hope and skepticism.

"I do," she replied, her voice firm. "Every day is an opportunity to start fresh, to build something new. You've lived in shadows long enough, Alaric. Let's bring light back into your life.".

His eyes softened, and he squeezed her hand back. "You make it sound so easy," he said, finally forcing a smile through the weight of his sorrow.

"Not ever," she said, with a playful glint in her eyes. "But I promise you, I will be right here beside you, helping you navigate every twist and turn.".

And now, their hands locked together as they walk; Alaric feels the heat of belief that has washed over him and lights the spark in him. "I get very little use to have someone at my side," he confessed in a return to vulnerability with his words.

"Well, it's about time," she shot back at him with all her playfulness and poise. "We are a team.

They laughed together, and the sound lightened the heavy air between them. It was a welcome respite, a glimpse into a future in which joy could exist along with their burdens. Together, they began to explore the ruins, Lyra's curiosity leading the way. She touched the stones reverently, listening intently as Alaric shared stories of the coven that had once thrived there.

This was the heart of our sanctuary, he said, pointing to a wide circular platform overgrown in moss. Here was where we performed our rites, binding us in ways that went beyond the merely physical.

"What sort of rites?" she asked with a look of wonder in her eyes.

Most were to honor the elements and our connection to the earth, he said, a faraway gaze crossing his face. We celebrated our existence, our immortality, and the bonds we shared. But there were also darker rituals, meant to protect us from the outside world.

Like what? she pressed, intrigued.

He hesitated, a shadow crossing his features. "Blood rituals," he finally admitted, his voice low. "To invoke protection from the coven's enemies. They were... necessary, but they left scars on our souls."

"Alaric, it's okay to let that go," she said gently, squeezing his hand. "You're not that person anymore. You can choose a different path.".

He nodded slowly, weighing her words. "I want to believe that," he said. "But old habits die hard."

Lyra smiled softly, her heart swelling with affection. "Then let's make new habits together. You have me by your side, remember?

And so, as they wandered, the forest came alive around them; whispers of the past from the rustling leaves and chirping crickets echoed in their ears. There was the beauty of the ruins-the testament to strength and survival, reminding Alaric that there is beauty in darkness.

They came to the grove's edge, where a little stream ran through the stones; the water sparkled with the moonlight. "This stream is life-giving," Alaric said, his eyes mirroring the shimmering water. "It once gave us sustenance for both body and soul.".

Lyra knelt beside the water, dipping her fingers into the cool, clear liquid. "It feels refreshing," she said, looking up at him. "Just like this place. It's a reminder that even in the darkest of shadows, there can be light."

Alaric watched her. His heart was welling up with a mix of emotions. "You have a way of seeing the world, Lyra. It is. beautiful.".

"Thank you," she said, a rosy blush spreading across her cheeks. "But it's not just me. It's the way you're beginning to see yourself too. I can see the light creeping in, Alaric. You're starting to let go of the darkness."

He felt the truth of her words reach down to him. "It's terrifying," he admitted. "Letting go of the past means confronting the pain I've buried for so long."

"But it also means making room for healing," she urged, her voice steady. "You can't carry it all forever. It's time to free yourself."

With a deep breath, Alaric stepped forward closer to the stream, examining his reflection in the silver moonlight. For the first time in a really long time, he was no longer looking at some kind of monster peering back from that glassy surface, but a man who'd been through hell and was slowly beginning to come out alive.

"I want to try," he said, his voice heavy with emotion. "I want to fight for this, for us."

Lyra beamed at him, her happiness contagious. "Then let's start right now. Together."

In

It was during this time that Lyra and Alaric stood side by side, entwining their fingers as they gazed into the shimmering water. Everything was alive, full of purpose and the promises of a new beginning. With the help of Lyra, he felt himself determined and strong.

He bent closer to the stream and whispered a silent vow of letting go of all his burdens and embracing the future. The water, flowing around them, seemed to take away the leftovers of his past, washing over him with a feeling of renewal.

And so, under the twinkling lights of the stars, they made a pact: A sanctuary, born of mutual dreams, hopes, and the indomitable tie they were forging between each other.

CHAPTER ELEVEN

THE GATHERING STORM

And their haven did not bring peace for long. Here Alaric stood along the stream as stillness faded away to unease at his own awareness. Lingered disturbance in air, change of the wood, alerted instincts in which he hadn't experienced any kind of warning feeling for decades-a dangerous vibration which felt as chills.

Alaric?" Lyra asked, noticing a shift in his expression. His brow furrowed as he scanned her face for any clue about the tightness that seemed to enclose him suddenly. "What is it?

He pauses, his senses leaping to heightened awareness, the forest around them springing to life, charged with energy he cannot and will not ignore. "We're not alone," he answers softly, seriously. Dread settles into his chest, memories of his old coven clawing their way out at the edges of his mind—the shadows he thought he'd left behind.

Even so, before he could manage a word, dark forms advanced out of the darkness, and stepped forward into moonlight, carrying an authority aura with them, the sight of which made his heart sink in his breast. He knew them now - they were part of his old coven: faces expressions of curious wariness, like a wolf pack closing in on the prey.

"Alaric," the leader said, his smooth voice laced with the undertone of disapproval. The flickering of the torchlight illuminated all the sharp angles of the face, revealing a hidden predator beneath a veneer of calm. "We have been looking for you."

Alaric bristled at the words that ignited anger within him, trying to keep his emotions in check. "I left for a reason," he shot back. "You have no right tracking me down.".

The eyes of the coven leader flickered to Lyra, appraising her presence with a mixture of disdain and suspicion. "And who is this?" he asked, his tone as cold as if the air around her was tainted. "A human? You know the rules, Alaric. Interacting with humans is a breach of our code."

Lyra took a step, the pounding of her heart within her chest. She heard all the animosity dripping from the coven people, but her determination steadied. "I come here for no trouble." She attempted to stand herself against the powerful presence by the coven. "I care for Alaric. He is not an ordinary vampire; he's a person."

"Person?" one of the other members sneered, a cruel smile twisting his lips. "You have no idea what you're dealing with. This is dangerous, and you have no place in our world."

Alaric instinctively stepped forward to put himself between Lyra and the coven, tensing his body. "Enough!" he growled, his veins buzzing with it. "I will not let you threaten her. She deserves to know the truth about me, and if you cannot accept that, then you have no claim over me."

The leader's face had set in a hard mask, a flicker of amusement playing on his lips as if Alaric's defiance were an entertaining spectacle. "You do not understand the consequences, Alaric. You continue down this path, risking exposing our existence to the world. We cannot allow that to happen.".

Conversation seemed heavy in the air, tense as a lead weight. She could feel the turmoil rolling inside Alaric and the flicker of fear in his eyes, having to confront what was, after all, reality regarding the coven's might. "What are you going to do?" she whispered, fear curling in her belly as she glanced up at the shadowy figures hovering behind him.

Alaric turned to her, desperation etched on his features. "I'll protect you, Lyra. I promise," he said, his voice cracking with determination though she could hear the shiver of uncertainty beneath.

But the leader of the coven showed no sign of softening, her expression unmoving and cold. "We will do what we must to protect our secrets, Alaric. Consider this a warning. Choose wisely.".

And with that, they turned and disappeared back into the shadows, their silhouettes melting into the darkness. Alaric and Lyra stood amidst the ruins, the weight of uncertainty hanging heavy between them. The air felt thick, charged with unspoken fears, and Lyra shivered, though the night was warm.

"What do we do now?" she asked, her voice barely above a whisper.

Alaric ran a hand through his hair, frustration building just beneath the surface. "I don't know," he admitted, his voice strained. "They won't stop until they feel their secrets are safe. They'll come back."

Lyra shivered. "What if they want to harm us? I won't be able to lose you. I won't let them take you from me." Even the idea of it shook her, and the chance of losing him was going to give her a physical shiver down her spine.

"They won't take you from me," he said to her, dripping with conviction. "Still, we cannot be foolhardy. They have no rules, and in defense, they are highly dangerous.".

They said nothing, the weight of what had transpired settling heavy on their shoulders. The safe haven they had so briefly found moments before now threatened in every shadow, and fragments of Alaric's past seeped back into their world.

"What do you know about them?" Lyra asked, seeking to glean answers from Alaric's dark eyes. "You must have some knowledge of their strengths and weaknesses.".

Alaric nodded slowly, furrowing his brow as he thought over her question. "The coven is powerful, steeped in ancient magic. They have abilities that far surpass mine-manipulating shadows, illusions, even controlling lesser vampires. They've been around for centuries, and their influence stretches far beyond what I ever imagined."

"But they're not invincible," Lyra said, her voice firm. "You escaped them once. You can do it again.".

He turned to her with a flicker of admiration in his eyes. "You are right. They might think they can control me, but they have underestimated my desire for freedom." He paused, his chest aflame with a mix of anger and fear. "I will no longer be a pawn in their game."

She took a step closer. "Then let's come up with a plan. We need to think ahead-anticipate their moves."

"What do you suggest?" Alaric asked, intrigued.

"Let's not stay in one spot for too long. We can use the woods to our advantage, create distractions, set traps. You know this terrain better than anyone," she said, racing her thoughts through a dozen options. "We can get the jump on them."

Alaric's features evened out, his pride welling inside his chest. "I've always fought alone. I'm not used to having someone at my back."

"Well, you are no longer alone," she continued, determination radiating off of her. "We're in this together."

With a newfound sense of direction, they began plotting strategy, their voices were hushed but filled with a sense of passion. In the ruins, they created their own map from where they were, planning to flee and hide in dense forests. Alaric recalled the old trails from where he had escaped those after him and together drew a plan.

The shadows of the trees crept inward, forming a cocoon that felt both protective and suffocating. A night full of woods stood alive with sound- the rustle and snap of twigs-till every inconsequential noise was magnified, echoing the storm churning in Alaric's heart.

Finally, they stepped back from the ruins, having outlined their strategy. "We should leave this place," Alaric said, scanning the treetops. "If they're searching for me, they'll come back here first."

Lyra nodded, a tightness in her chest. "But where do we go?"

Alaric gazed outward, toward the horizon, as the first lights of dawn began to brush the sky. "I know a cave, not far from here," he said. "It is hidden; we might be able to use it again. We can get out of here, make plans, and decide our next course of action there."

They trailed into the underbrush, where, lit by the thin light of dawn straining through the trees, they forced their footsteps. Alaric felt his past trudge behind him, a dark shadow, but with Lyra at his side came the smallest flicker of hope—a small but potent light that struggled against the solidity of the dark, overwhelming bulk.

Alaric," Lyra said, breaking the silence as they navigated the winding trail. "What if they find us? What if we can't get away?"

He turned to her, determination etched into his features. "Then we'll fight. I won't let them take you from me.".

Lyra's heart was pounding at the depth in his voice, with conviction running through him like a current. "I believe you," she said firmly, her own determination drawing strength. "Together, we can face whatever happens.".

With each step, they penetrated deeper into the woods, the sanctuary of the ruins receding behind. Alaric led the way, with heightened senses, the hairs on the back of his neck prickling with an awareness of danger lying just beyond their reach.

They were aware of the world that had now changed before them; denser woods grew, tangled in a protecting fence in front of them, while Alaric ran with his mind racing at each move they made, the rustling of leaves now making one warn that they were far from being safe.

Getting near to the cave brought relief along with it.

They finally washed over Alaric. He motioned her to go in ahead. His heart swelled inside him as he viewed his daughter's courage at times like these. Inside it was cool and black while the world outside poured the whole solar system with its burning splendor. Alaric felt the weight of it all press down against himself, but here perhaps lay their hope.

"We will figure this out," he promised, settling down next to her inside the cave. "We will do it one step at a time."

Lyra rested her head against him. He could feel her warmth help keep him grounded in a chaos that was churning his mind. "And what if they come?" she asked, the fragility in her voice almost drawing him in.

Alaric tightened his hold on her shoulder, resolve beginning to harden inside his chest. "Then we shall be ready for them together."

Outside, a storm gathered in the distance, but there in the cave was found another haven, this where hope flickered to lighten shadows of uncertainty. With it, they prepared together, preparing for the storm brewing within and outside them and what dangers lay in waiting; all this while propelled by the strength of their bond as well as the promise of brighter days ahead.

CHAPTER TWELVE

ULTIMATUM IN SHADOWS

The weight of the coven's visit was crushing down on Alaric. The storm raging inside him matched the one outside. The ultimatum hung over his head like a dark cloud, threatening to shatter the fragile peace they had built. He knew the risks of his connection with Lyra, but now it seemed the stakes were higher than ever.

As he paced restlessly in the woods, the threat of the coven loomed large, heavy as the shadows cast by the trees. "End your relationship with her," the leader had warned, his voice echoing in Alaric's mind. "Or face the consequences." The thought of leaving Lyra was unbearable, but the weight of the threat was almost too much to bear.

The moon was low and the leaves danced in the night breeze, their shadows shimmering in the silver light, but Alaric felt none of it. Anxiety crept into every breath he took as every heartbeat echoed the turmoil that surged within him. For centuries he had run from the dark forces of his past, and now they were crashing back into his life with a vengeance.

Knowledge of what was to come led Alaric to practice old skills he had thought he'd left buried in the past. He continued to keep practicing in secret, holding onto his abilities as a lifeline that might protect Lyra. In the quiet woods, he moves fluid, fierce and every strike, every evasion reminding him of battles fought alone. Every movement danced with shadows because his body reminded him of the old life he had tried so hard to leave behind. Nothing, however, could keep him from defending her at all costs.

Sweat beaded on his forehead as he ran, combining with the forest earth smells to fill his nostrils. Memories of the coven flooded his mind:

blood oaths, rituals, and betrayals. Every recollection spurred him forward, fueling the fire of his resolve. He could not—would not—let them drag him back into their dark fold. Lyra was his light, the spark that had reignited a part of him long thought extinguished.

She realized though that the more Alaric practiced, the more she felt his turmoil inside. Not too long afterwards, she went to him again; her eyes peeling into his, a tempest of concern brewing behind them. "You've been distant again," she said softly yet firmly. "Please, Alaric, talk to me. I can't take this silence between us anymore.".

He could n't speak, his mind divided between protecting her from such truth and wanting to burden her with everything. It felt as though words now hung in his mouth-a weight that he couldn't possibly bear. "I could n't risk getting you in the way, Lyra," he muttered over his shoulder, trying his best not to break any of his own bonds at that particular moment as final wisps of light pierced the gaps between the trunks.

"Then let me decide for myself," she pressed, moving closer, her resolve unshakeable. "I deserve to know the truth."

Alaric's heart twisted painfully as he felt the weight of her gaze. Trust radiated from her eyes, making it harder to turn away. "You wouldn't want to know if it meant putting your life at risk," he countered, his heart aching with the burden of the secret he carried.

Stop covering me by pushing me away," she pleaded, her voice heavy with emotion. "I want to be with you, Alaric. I won't let fear dictate our relationship.

The strength of her conviction had momentarily broken through Alaric's defenses. He wanted to tell her everything, share the burden of his past, but fear gripped him like a vice. "I don't want you to see me as a monster," he said, his voice barely above a whisper. "But that's what I am. I'm a threat to you."

Lyra moved forward, so that the space between them was gone, and she felt the warmth that radiated from his body. "You're not a monster to me," she said in a strong tone, going for his hand, and her touch triggered a flame of hope within him. "You're still Alaric I care for, and I won't believe you are incapable of being something greater.".

It was there, standing under the vast expanse of stars, that Alaric felt a flicker of hope ignite within him. Lyra's conviction and courage were a balm to his wounded spirit, and he began to realize she was right. He could not protect her by shutting her out; he needed to let her in, even if it terrified him.

"Okay," he finally said, drawing a quivering breath. "I will tell you. You must promise me, however, that you'll take care. What I have to share with you does not only pertain to me; it is part of you too."

Lyra nodded steadily. She looked resolute. "I promise, Alaric. I can do it."

Alaric took a step back, collecting his thoughts as he searched for the right words. "The coven I left... they are not just a group of vampires. They are ancient, powerful, and they don't take kindly to betrayal. When I chose to leave, I was severing ties with them—ties that come with serious consequences."

Lyra listened intently, her heart racing as she absorbed his words. "What kind of consequences?

"They want me back," he said, the pain of the past bearing heavily within his voice. "And they're willing to do whatever it takes in order to get me. They've given me an ultimatum: end our relationship, or they will come after you."

Shocks washed over her. An anger so fierce boiled into full view. "They think they can threaten us? They don't get to decide who you love, Alaric!

He gripped her hand harder, trying to soothe her. "I know it doesn't feel fair, but they do not care about that. They will not care twice. I cannot let them harm you because of me."

Lyra's eyes glinted with defiance. "You don't decide what we risk and what we don't in this. I love you, Alaric. And I am not going to let them run my life.

His heart swelling by her words, still above him a dark shadow lingered. "You have no idea the depth of power they possess. They would use dark magic on you, to harm you; I won't permit them to do so." She declared in the flame in her spirit, like burning fire, "Then we shall fight back! Let's not let them threaten us.".

Alaric was full of amazement at how determined she was to face what had brought the danger that lay before her. "You are bold, Lyra, but you mustn't do this; it is a burden."

"I want to be there with this, Alaric. If we will ever be able to stay together then I have to learn what is out there before us. She spoke very softly to him, this time sincerity poured from each word as she said with great intensity: "Let me help you.".

For a moment, Alaric did not move; he hesitated between respect for her bravery and instinct to safeguard her. "I will not let them harm you," he declared finally, his voice heavy with conviction. "But if we are to do this, we must prepare ourselves. We need to seek allies and ways to protect ourselves.".

"I have some ideas," Lyra said, her excitement clear. "I've been reading up on local legend and I think we could try to find some old manuscripts that might be able to tell us more about the coven and their vulnerabilities."

Alaric couldn't help but grin at her spirited suggestion, a beacon in the bleakness of their situation. "That's a good starting point. But we're going to need some weaponry too: something to keep us alive."

"Then let's take what we can," she said, determination in her voice. "I'll ask everyone I can. We can't let them choose for us."

And as they started making plans, a darkness seemed to settle atop them. The woods themselves seemed to breathe secrets of danger and of promise, and the rustling of leaves echoed the risks taken.

"Remember," Alaric said, his face growing serious, "if we're going to do this, we have to be careful. The coven will be watching, waiting for any sign of weakness. We can't let them know what we're planning."

Lyra nodded, her face set in determination. "I can be careful. I won't let them see me coming. We'll use the shadows to our advantage."

When the first rays of dawn broke through the canopy, hope in Alaric crept from the shadows of darkness. Together they would face the ultimatum of the coven and protect Lyra at any cost. It was through their bond that they could hold strong; though shadows stood large before them, fear would not dictate their destiny.

For the next few days, they labored without rest, amassing knowledge and resources. Lyra plunged into old texts and folklore, stories of strength and resilience against dark forces. Alaric contacted old allies, those who understood the dangers they faced, gathering a network of support to help protect Lyra and stand against the coven.

Their nights had been filled with whispered plans and shared fears, and laughter and hope. It was in those nights preparing for the inevitable confrontation that Alaric found solace in Lyra's indomitable spirit, which lit up even the darkest corners of his past.

But beneath the surface, the storm brewed. Alaric could feel the coven's presence lurking in the shadows, their eyes on him, and the weight of their ultimatum pressing heavily upon his chest. He had to remain vigilant, to protect

Lyra at all costs, for he knew that the shadows held dangers he could not yet comprehend.

But with Lyra by his side, he had a new sense of purpose. Together they'll face the shadows and become stronger, ready to withstand anything that the coven may be throwing their way. Finally, when the preparations were almost over, Alaric looked at Lyra, and his heart swelled up with determination.

We will face them together," he promised, knowing in any case they wouldn't retreat. The bond they had forged would be his shield, and together they would face the gathering storm.

CHAPTER THIRTEEN

LUNAR ECLIPSE

Lyra's pulse quickened as she took in the chaos around her. Alaric moved with grace and power, his body a whirlwind of motion as he deflected blows and countered attacks from the coven. Each strike he landed echoed with the weight of his resolve, but the sheer number of enemies pressed down on him like a dark cloud, suffocating their chances of victory.

"Alaric!" she shouted, desperation creeping into her voice. "What do we do? We can't hold them off like this!"

He glanced back at her, his eyes fierce but filled with an undercurrent of fear. "We need to find a way to separate the leader from the others. If we can do that, we stand a chance." His voice was urgent, each word laced with the tension of their dire situation.

Lyra nodded, her determination hardening. She had seen how the coven leader wielded power over his followers, how his very presence seemed to command the shadows. "Then we'll go after him together!"

Alaric hesitated for a moment, concern etched across his features. "No, Lyra, I can't risk you getting hurt. Stay behind me!"

But Lyra refused to cower, her heart swelling with courage. "You're not getting rid of me that easily! We're stronger together."

With that, they fought side by side, Lyra drawing on her newfound resolve. She had spent weeks learning about the dark forces they were up against and the vulnerabilities of the coven. The power she had felt coursing through her veins during their training surged again, a reminder that she was more than just an ordinary human. She could be a force for good, a light in the darkness.

As Alaric engaged with the nearest attacker, Lyra focused on a second enemy approaching from the side. She swung her arm out, using the wooden stake she had hastily fashioned earlier from a fallen branch. The stake connected with the vampire's chest, piercing through the fabric of his cloak. The creature hissed in surprise as it stumbled back, momentarily disoriented.

"Nice shot!" Alaric called out, a flicker of pride lighting his eyes as he dispatched another opponent with a swift kick.

With renewed confidence, Lyra pressed forward, moving with Alaric as they fought against the tide of shadows. The forest around them echoed with the sounds of battle—the clash of bodies, the low growls of their adversaries, and the rustle of leaves disturbed by their frantic movements.

"Let's push toward the leader!" Alaric shouted over the din. They fought their way through the chaos, focusing on the flickering figure of the coven leader, whose dark robes billowed ominously as he directed his minions with effortless authority.

Just as they began to make their way through the throng, the leader caught sight of them, his eyes narrowing with malevolent intent. "You think you can defy me?" he sneered, raising his hands, summoning the shadows around him like a dark shroud. "I will show you the true meaning of power!"

The air crackled with energy as he unleashed a wave of dark magic, tendrils of shadow snaking toward them. Alaric instinctively pushed Lyra back, shielding her with his body. "Get down!" he shouted, and she obeyed, ducking behind a tree as the wave of darkness crashed against it, splintering the wood and sending shards flying.

"Alaric!" she cried, fear clawing at her throat as she saw him stagger under the weight of the magic. But he quickly regained his footing, determination blazing in his eyes.

"Stay low!" he yelled, recovering his composure. "We need to find cover and regroup. We can't let him isolate us!"

Lyra's heart raced as she watched him move with purpose. She could feel the bond between them strengthening, a tether of love and courage that whispered to her to keep fighting. With each breath, she harnessed the energy around her, focusing on the knowledge she had gained from her research. The stories of the coven's weaknesses swirled in her mind, urging her forward.

"Alaric, we need to distract him!" she yelled, her voice cutting through the chaos. "If we can draw his attention away, we can catch him off guard!"

He met her gaze, his eyes filled with fierce resolve. "I'll create a diversion. When I do, you go for him. Aim for the heart!"

Lyra nodded, her heart pounding as she watched him move. Alaric sprinted toward a cluster of shadows, drawing the attention of several coven members. "Over here!" he shouted, his voice ringing out with challenge. "You want me? Come and get me!"

The coven members hesitated, caught off guard by his boldness. Seizing the moment, Alaric launched himself at them, engaging in fierce combat. The shadows surged forward, drawn to him like moths to a flame.

"Now, Lyra!" he called out, his voice strained yet determined.

With a surge of adrenaline, she raced toward the leader, dodging debris and leaping over fallen branches. The darkness twisted around her, but she pushed through, focused on the target ahead. The leader's back was turned, momentarily distracted by Alaric's fierce onslaught.

She lunged forward, the wooden stake gripped tightly in her hand. "This ends now!" she shouted, plunging the stake toward his heart with all her strength.

The leader turned just in time, but it was too late. The stake pierced through the fabric of his cloak, connecting with his chest. A howl of rage erupted from him, reverberating through the night like thunder. The shadows around him recoiled, as if in fear of their master's imminent demise.

Lyra felt a rush of exhilaration, but it was quickly tempered by a sense of urgency as the leader staggered backward, his eyes blazing with fury. "You think you can defeat me, little girl?" he spat, venom dripping from his words. "You have no idea what you've unleashed!"

Before she could react, he raised a hand, summoning the shadows back to him. Dark tendrils slashed toward Lyra, aiming to ensnare her. Just as they closed in, Alaric broke free from his fight, rushing to her side. He intercepted the shadows with a fierce strike, his determination unwavering.

"Lyra, move!" he shouted, and she darted aside just as Alaric thrust his arm out, sending the shadows spiraling away from them.

Together, they fought through the chaotic remnants of the battle, drawing on their bond and the strength of their love. As the coven leader regrouped, his fury palpable, Alaric turned to Lyra, his voice filled with urgency. "We need to finish this, together."

With a nod, Lyra felt a rush of power flowing through her. The stories she had learned, the power of the lunar eclipse, all came together in a rush of clarity. "We can use the eclipse against him!" she exclaimed, her heart racing with possibility.

The moon had shifted to a deep crimson hue, the eclipse casting an otherworldly glow over the forest. Lyra remembered the lore she had studied: the eclipse was a time of reckoning, a chance to banish darkness and reclaim light.

"Alaric, we can channel the energy of the eclipse! Together, we can harness its power!"

He met her gaze, the determination in his eyes igniting a fire within her. "Let's do it."

They positioned themselves, forming a line of defense against the advancing shadows. Alaric focused on the energy flowing through him, drawing on the strength of the moon and the bond they shared. Lyra mirrored his actions, closing her eyes and breathing deeply, feeling the energy of the eclipse resonate within her.

The coven leader snarled, sensing their intentions. "You think a mere lunar event can save you?" he scoffed, raising his hands in defiance. "I will crush you both!"

But as he unleashed another wave of dark magic, Alaric and Lyra stood firm, their connection amplifying the energy swirling around them. They combined their strengths, channeling the power of the eclipse through their bodies.

"Now!" Alaric shouted, thrusting his arm forward as they unleashed a wave of light that surged toward the leader, a blinding beacon cutting through the darkness.

The coven leader's eyes widened in shock as the light enveloped him, displacing the shadows that had shielded him. "No!" he screamed, his voice filled with rage and fear as the power of the eclipse broke through his defenses. The shadows recoiled, dissipating into nothingness.

With a final surge, the light exploded around them, engulfing the leader in its brilliance. The air crackled with energy as the dark magic unraveled, the malevolence that had pervaded the grove beginning to dissipate. Alaric and Lyra stood resolute, united in their determination as the eclipse reached its zenith.

As the darkness lifted, the coven members faltered, their confidence shattered in the face of the power they had underestimated. Alaric and Lyra exchanged glances, the bond between them shining brighter than ever before.

"Now's our chance!" Alaric urged, his voice ringing with newfound strength. They pushed forward, launching themselves at the remaining coven members, using the momentum of their victory to drive them back.

The chaos of the night unfolded around them, but they were no longer fighting alone. They were a force to be reckoned with, fueled by love and resilience. As they pressed onward, the tide turned, the coven's hold over the shadows

waning.

In that moment, Lyra felt a sense of freedom wash over her. They were no longer just survivors; they were warriors, ready to reclaim their destiny. Together, they would stand against the darkness, illuminating the path ahead.

As the lunar eclipse waned, the shadows retreated, leaving only the echoes of their confrontation behind. Alaric and Lyra emerged from the battle, battered but unbroken, their spirits entwined in the glow of the moonlight. The path ahead was uncertain, but they faced it together, ready to confront whatever challenges lay ahead in the shadows of Oak Hollow.

CHAPTER FOURTEEN

A BLADE OF SILVER

The battle raged on, the clearing now assuming a kaleidoscope pattern of light and shadow. Lyra's pendant blazed with a fierce inner flame, radiating warmth and energy that engulfed her and Alaric, pushing back the darkening waves. With each swing of Alaric's arm and each pulse of energy from the pendant, they cut a swath through the ranks of the coven, sending shadows running like wind-blown leaves.

"Move on!" Alaric screamed, his voice a shout against the din. He delivered a swift kick to another coven member, and darkness closed in around him as they pushed forward into the melee. Lyra remained close, her heart thumping with excitement and terror, the power of the pendant anchoring her to the turmoil.

In her mind, while fighting, came the recollections of stories that her grandmother used to tell: stories of bravery and tenacity, of how the pendant protected their family when it was threatened. Every one of those memories pushed her forward with renewed willpower, making a fire that would never be quenched. And every attack that they managed to fend off made her feel a sense of closeness to her lineage and the women who had borne the pendant before her.

Lyra! Yonder! Alaric shouted, pointing toward an encircling crowd of coven followers gathering their fallen head, who seemed to be recovering from her assault on him earlier. The shadows writhed in agitation and contorted upon their bodies in a melee of wrath and confusion: "We must break their ranks!

Lyra nodded, the determination in her growing as they moved in unison. Alaric led the charge, his body being a shield as he parried blows from the coming shadows. Lyra held the pendant aloft; its light illuminated their way. As they closed in to the leader, she saw the fury etched in his face, a desperation rage that only grew harder as he realized the pendant's power.

"Do you really think that trinket can save you?" he sneered, gathering darkness around him like a cloak. "I'll enjoy watching you fail!"

Lyra focused on the pendant, which was surging in heat with her emotions. "We won't fail," she declared, trying to sound strong even as fear churned inside of her. "We have the strength of our ancestors with us!"

That adrenaline rush pushed them forward as they sprinted through what was left of the coven members. Lyra felt the energy in the beat of the pendant pulsating with Alaric's movements; that was pure light and intent. She charged with the rest now, her footsteps exuding poise.

As they closed in, the dark energy was let loose. Tendrils moved in at speed and ferocity. Alaric launched into quick reflexes and threw an arm outwards. Energy snapped back on itself with an enormous hit. The light clashed with dark magic, and an explosion that seemed to reach all of the clearing as brilliant rays erupted.

"Now it's Lyra's turn!" he said, desperate in a hurry.

Lyra took a step forward and poured all her energy into the pendant, which then brightened up. She threw it forward toward the leader, and the light spread into a brilliant beam cutting through the shadows that shrouded him. Darkness quivered, and for a moment, the leader was taken aback by the force he had not anticipated.

No!" he shouted, contorting his face in rage as he shielded himself from the radiant energy. Too late: the light swept over him, bathing the clearing in a fiery glow.

Lyra felt a surge of triumph as shadows began to retreat, shrinking in the rigors of the pendant's power. Coven members hesitated, nervously casting glances at their leader now caught in a cocoon of light.

"Forward!" shouted Alaric, gaining in momentum from the triumph unrolling. Together, they charge forward, the pulse of their hearts beat now synchronized for the same cause. Each blow and strike by the pendant hurtles them backward, a coven member at every blow creating an open way towards the leader.

As Lyra came closer, she could see the desperation written across his face. He lunged at her, trying to call up the shadows, and then they recoiled from the light cast by the pendant, unwilling to come near its strength. "You think you can stop this? You are nothing!" he bellowed, in anguish.

Perhaps we mean nothing to you," Alaric returned hotly, his words burning, as he moved to Lyra's other side. "But together, we are far more than you could possibly imagine!

With one final spurt of energy, Lyra and Alaric flung themselves toward the leader. The pendant blazed with an all-consuming intensity, dispelling the shadows that clung to him. As she approached, Lyra held up the pendant, feeling energy course through her, intertwined with her love for Alaric and their task.

"Let's put an end to this!" Lyra screamed, holding the pendant up toward the leader.

The light burst out from the pendant, bathing him. A shrill scream exploded from the leader's mouth as the light engulfed him, dismantling the darkness that ruled the forest. The shadows that guarded him retreated and dissipated into wisps as the radiant energy poured over them.

The light slowly faded away, and the clearing remained silent. The members of the coven scattered off, their faces etched with fear as they darted into the depths of the forest, leaving their dark allegiance behind. Lyra and Alaric stood in the clearing, gasping for air, wide-eyed, as the aftermath of the battle washed over them.

"Did we..." Lyra panted her words to Alaric, her heart racing.

I guess we did," he was saying, his voice still full of amazement and relief. They both sat there in stunned silence, their bodies vibrating through the last of their fight.

As the last vestiges of darkness receded, Lyra felt the pendant chill against her palm, and its glow dimmed but did not extinguish. She could feel the energy still swirling around them, reminding her of the bond that had fueled their victory.

"Lyra," Alaric said, his expression softening as he stepped closer. "You were incredible. I couldn't have done this without you."

She smiled. Her heart had become full and swollen by pride and affection. "We did it, Alaric. We are strong as a team."

Now, in this moment they realized the extent of what connected them- something ignited in fire and light- they stood firm together with whatever was about to cross their path while the earliest shades of dawn spread and colored the horizon in golden and orange tints. Darkness would retreat for now, but the real fight was only just beginning. Together, they would unravel all that was left unknown, ready to face whatever lay in the future for them in Oak Hollow.

BLOOD AND BOND

Alaric and Lyra fought side by side, turning the clearing around them into a battleground where the clash of darkness and light ignited fierce energy. Every movement they made was imbued with the resonance of their blood bond, a connection that went beyond the physical realm and deepened their understanding of one another. They became a symphony of strength, their hearts pulsing in harmony as they faced the coven together.

Refreshed by vigor, Alaric charged forward, moving like a whirlwind of determined fury. With each strike, he poured powerful energy from their shared blood. Shadows that had seemed insurmountable now faltered before their combined might. Lyra's fierce spirit, Alaric felt, ignited his resolve as they moved in perfect sync to defend each other instinctively.

Stay close!" Alaric yelled, adrenaline pumping into his veins as they stared down the nearest coven member. He parried an incoming strike with one arm, using the other to swing a fierce blow that sent the attacker sprawling backward into the darkness. His strength was amplified by the feel of their bond, adding to his instincts as he fought with her.

Lyra, equally empowered, threw a swing of her determination to strike out, but her pendant was still aflame in her hand. "Let's show them what we can do!" she shouted, her voice resonating with confidence, moving towards Alaric and as she did to get by his side; her pendant pulsed her spirit into creating bursts of lights illuminating the shadows about them.

As every step brought him closer to them, he could see shadows moving back and the evil figures shrinking as more power was drawn forth from the couple. Alaric could feel the coven members' hearts trembling with fear as they realized wicked confidence was melting away with each drop of strength drawn in blood and sacrifice between them. "We're stronger together!" he declared, feeling it true within him.

A new force seemed to course through his veins as he recalled Lyra offering him her blood; warmth seemed to infuse every fiber of his being from the shared essence of himself and the other, but a fire burned in his chest as he was thrust ahead. He could see his own unyielding spirit reflected in the way she fought, and this drove him with an even deeper sense of purpose.

"Let's push them back!" Lyra shouted, her voice carrying above the noise as they launched into a coordinated attack. Alaric could feel the beat of their bond guiding their movements, silent communication that flowed between them as they exchanged blows, dodged strikes, and fought back the encroaching darkness.

As they moved, the shadows around them began to falter, their dark forms shifting uneasily as they faced the duo's radiant energy. The pendant, infused with Lyra's love and sacrifice, sent ripples of light that danced across the clearing, illuminating the faces of their attackers. The coven members exchanged nervous glances, the confidence of their numbers faltering under the intensity of the light.

"Now!" Alaric yelled, leaping into the window of opportunity as several members of the coven glanced around at one another, briefly distracted. He and Lyra launched themselves together, a storm of fury and intent.

Lyra swung the pendant in, and the light leaped forth in a blinding burst that sent the closest of the attackers tumbling over their heads. "This is for all the times you have hid in the shadows!" she yelled, her voice full of holy wrath. "You're not going to take our light!

As the light enveloped all the members of the coven, Alaric could feel the warmth of Lyra's courage blending into his own, bringing power into the very air they breathed. Darkness recoiled, unsure how to contend with the vibrant energy that they had become.

"No more running!" Alaric cried out, stabbing an assailant down as the ring of the blade into the open was metallic. "It ends here!

And yet, with this resumption, they stepped forth into a further depth of struggle. There beside him, Lyra's spirit - valiant as she stood, striking each thrust sharp and with immense strength as every blow he launched seemed to emit her might, the darkness cast upon darkness rolled back into place.

And, drawn in from the circle of the clearing's edge, the others in this coven stood again formed, master at the front, his eyes seething furiously. "Any idea you would be our conquerors?" he hurled shadows swirling around him like dark storms, encircling, "You nothing! This home!

She could hardly breathe with the thought of him before her, but she held her ground by Alaric's side, his energy strengthening her. "We're not afraid of you!" she cried out, holding the pendant aloft. The glow intensified, as if in reaction to her words. "You have terrorized Oak Hollow long enough. Your reign of darkness must end!

With that declaration, the pendant began to glow and Alaric could feel the energy start to swell inside him: the power of their bond reverberating through each fibre of his body. Alaric looked at Lyra. They nodded to each other in a silent promise of solidarity and strength.

Together!" Alaric yelled and, with their hearts bound together, they flung themselves at the leader, a bolt of light shooting from the pendant as they lunged in unison.

The leader raised his hands and created a dark barrier to shield himself from Alaric and Lyra, who pressed onward, the pendant lighting up their way. They charged through with fierce determination, the strength of their bond shattering the shadows like glass.

The clearing erupted in a blinding flash as their light surged forward, engulfing the leader and illuminating the surrounding woods. For a moment, everything was silent—an awe-inspiring stillness that settled over the battlefield as the light expanded, illuminating the faces of the remaining coven members, who stood frozen in shock.

And when the light faded, the leader stumbled back, his eyes wide with incredulity. "How is this possible?" he gasped, his voice now shaking with fear rather than the arrogance that had defined him before.

"It's love," Lyra said, her voice steady and unwavering. "It's the bond we've forged through sacrifice and trust. You underestimated us!

One last push and they had fully unleashed their connection-the pendant radiating with the essence of their shared strength. The shadows that thrived in darkness faltered and started to dissipate as they retreated into the heart of the forest.

Together, Alaric and Lyra came out on top from the battle as a bright warm glow illuminated the clearing, a testament to the unbreakable bond that they shared. The two stood together, beating hearts pounding in their chests and inhaling the aftermath of chaos.

As the very first rays of sunlight managed to peek through the trees to paint the clearing in its golden hue, they realized they had won the darkness not only for themselves as one entity. Alaric looked at Lyra and his heart was brimming with gratitude and love. "You saved me, Lyra," he whispered, the weight of their journey settling between them.

"And you saved me, Alaric," she whispered softly, her eyes shining with pride and love. They knew at that moment that their bond had been altered forever, the blood they shared entwining their destinies into one, a promise of love and strength for whatever was to come.

Hand in hand, they turned toward the dawn, ready to face their future together, knowing they would stand as one against the darkness for all eternity.

CHAPTER SIXTEEN

BENEATH THE CRIMSON MOON

The total lunar eclipse was at its height, and the chaos of war was at its loudest. The clearing echoed with snarls and growls, thick air heavy with sweat and fear as the coven clashed with growing ferocity. They knew they were being pushed back by Alaric and Lyra's combined strength. Yet instead of weakening, Alaric and Lyra stood firm, united in their determination to protect each other and their home.

Alaric's chest pounded against the battle, energy from their bond running wildly through his veins. However, amidst this chaos, something nagged at his brain. He could feel this power every strike he made brought him but it came at a steep price. He felt his choices weighed upon him-a constant reminder that staying with Lyra could only lead to more danger for her. The fear of what he might lose clawed at him, gnawing at the edges of his resolve.

Alaric, in the midst of chaos, spied Lyra fighting beside him; her eyes fierce and unwavering. She shouted over the din of war. "Alaric!" "Don't you dare think about leaving me behind!"

These were the words that struck like lightning and set ablaze her fire. Lyra, in her bold spirit, showed confidence and knew there was a fight going inside him. "Remember what we are fighting for," she urged him, a determination in her eyes. "Our love is our best strength. Together, there's nothing we can't face."

The leader of the coven then suddenly stepped out from the dark. His eyes glinted with an edge as he stood before them. It was a move perhaps for the fourth or the fifth time, yet none seemed to recognize the act. "Think you deny us?" he sneered, venom dripping off of every word. "Oh, fool,

Alaric. All nature was given up to all his instincts for what? Love that passed as a swift wind?"

In that confusion and chaos, the darkness swirling around him rooted him to Lyra. "No," he said, his voice even as he faced the leader, "I have found my strength, and it is because of her. You cannot take that from me.".

Those words ignited a desperate fight between them. In Alaric's own word, Alaric and Lyra moved into combat together, their steps slick, in sync, so much power in the blood pendant, so much shared bond that it became possible to almost feel it, touch it, and then its pulse would spread out so far that it became one protection, pushing back attacks of the coven back onto themselves, freeing those combatants from the threats of being overwhelmed.

With each stroke and counterclock, Alaric felt that power of their love embraced them, reviving his spirit. They struck side by side against the coven members with a force that seemed to emanate from a common goal. Shadows sought to close around them, but with each blow, the darkness retreated as the light of their union prevailed.

The fighting continued and the shadows started to retreat, their forms fading out into the pendant's light. Renewed purpose began stirring within Alaric as his love for Lyra lit a fire that fueled his will to survive, making the battle more about saving their life and their future together rather than just survival.

Together!" Alaric yelled, and with their combined hearts they shot a wave of strength to slam the coven leader into the ground. Alaric could feel the fight shift; their love mixed with the power of the pendant created a wall around them from the shadows.

At that moment, Dawn's crack came, and sunlight went over the treetops into the clearing, painting a golden, warm glow of light. The eclipse receded, and it seemed obvious that the members of the coven couldn't win. With one final hiss of anger, they retreated into the depths of the forest, where the dark forms melted into the shadows.

Alaric and Lyra stood, battered but triumphant, their hearts pounding with adrenaline as they surveyed the devastation of battle. They faced the darkness and in the process had come to build a bond no one would ever be able to break-a bond to guide them over any obstacle yet to be encountered.

"We did it, Lyra," Alaric said softly, turning toward her, half in awe and half in relief. "We fended them off.

Her eyes gleamed with triumph, but beneath it lay an undercurrent of vulnerability. "We did it together," she whispered softly, moving closer to him, her hands slightly shaking as they reached for each other's warmth. "I couldn't have done it without you.".

So then as they embrace, sunshine spread out upon the broadened Oak Hollow sky because they chased all the night from their face and shadows into a whole light on which they found that there had been light for conquering shadows to make path after going into dawn, illuminated, and bright.

The battle had shaped inside them a new strength; the bond will guide them into whatever danger comes their way. And they saw the sunrise together, knowing that love is the biggest tool they could possibly use to face the future unknown.

Yet, standing there in golden light, Alaric cannot help but feel the old doubts linger. He meets Lyra's eyes across the battlefield, where so recently they had fought at each other's side—love and pride in spilling blood, fear mixed with love. He will speak to her of such thoughts.

"Lyra," he said hesitantly, "I wish to talk of what has come to pass tonight. Concerning us."

Her expression changed to one of worry. "What is it, Alaric? You can tell me anything."

He took a deep breath. The weight of his words hung between them. "I know that our bond has made me stronger, but I couldn't shake the feeling that staying with me would just bring more danger into your life. The coven will not stop hunting us. You've seen how far they will go.

Lyra stepped back half a step, her eyes locked on his. "You think I'd be safer without you? Alaric, I chose this. I chose to fight with you because I believe in us. I believe in our love."

"But it's not just about us," he said, his voice thick with emotion. "I can't bear the thought of losing you to this darkness. It's too much to ask of you.".

"Love isn't about asking for safety; it's about standing together against the storm," she said, her eyes unwavering. "I'm not afraid of the danger. I'm afraid of losing you if you try to protect me by pushing me away."

Her words pierced the veil of doubt that had shrouded his heart. Alaric could see the truth shining in her eyes, a fierce light that matched the glow of the pendant still hanging between them. "I won't leave you," he said, feeling the warmth of her determination wrap around him like a lifeline. "I need you, Lyra. You are my strength.".

And you are mine, she said, moving closer, as their heartbeats matched. Together we'll go and face whatever comes our way. Together always.

With the sun rising above, casting its golden glow across their entwined forms, Alaric began to feel the weight of his doubt lifting. They had faced the shadows and come out on top; their love would continue guiding them through the trials yet to come. In that moment, under the warmth of dawn, he made silent vows to cherish and protect their bond, knowing together they could face anything-darkness and light alike.

CHAPTER SEVENTEEN

FAREWELL TO DARKNESS

As the dawn broke over the aftermath of the fierce fight, Alaric walked mindlessly, almost aimlessly on the hill overlooking Oak Hollow. The night had been crazy, full of commotion and uncertainty, but as the first light crept over the horizon, this was probably going to be his last sunrise ever. The sky was an oranges-and-pinks-and-purple tapestry in a gentle fade from one to the next, painting the sky in splendorous beauty. Yet to Alaric, all this glory was tinged with profound sorrow, reminding him of his life as a vampire: loneliness, loss, and memory echoes that refused to go away. He thought of friendships lost over the centuries, of laughter shared now impossible to locate in time, and of Lyra, whom he would lose. The weight of existence bore down on him. He felt an overwhelming feeling of finality, one in which the sun could seal his fate, an end to an era where he had learned to care and all the possible loss of all this again.

With the sun yet to resurface from its hiding horizon, Alaric's eyes closed in and invited the memories over him in waves. In those early years, he used to be an adolescent as a vampire where the sensation of immortality was mainly overpowered by the severe loneliness it triggered. Here, he recalls nights full of wild laughter while he was going through exhilaration in his youth with all the vigor of every moment, each of it being bittersweet for him. Friends had faded from his life like shadows of dawn, faces growing misty specters in the brain as the years flowed past. Every memory now held a blend of delight with pain, and joyous laughter echoed through hollow places in his heart. And then when he looked upon Lyra, as this strange light, within him he knew things moved. He thought of the moments they had shared—the way she ignited a flame inside him that he had long thought was extinguished. With her, he had felt alive for the first time in centuries, and the thought of losing that vitality pierced him with an ache deeper than any physical wound. At this point of reflection, he was able to feel a moment of peace, knowing that he had fought for something worth saving, for love that transcended life and death.

Alaric was lost in his thoughts when he suddenly sensed a gentle presence beside him. He turned and found Lyra standing quietly. Her figure was silhouetted against the rising sun. She looked unearthly, almost celestial. It was as though the light that started to come on in the world around them had somehow been lit within her. Alaric knew she felt the turmoil inside of him; it wasn't necessary for her to speak the words-she felt it every bit as sharply as he did. The weight of his fear hung between them. Then turning to her, his full heart swelling with love and fear, in that one moment of vulnerability, the world was awakened all around them, and he could confess all his deepest fears: losing her, seeing darkness creep back into their lives, and his near fate. Her eyes met his steadily and firmly as she looked up, her eyes full of assurance that nothing the darkness had brought could be more powerful than their bond. She reached out to grasp his hand, drawing his attention to her warmth as she anchored him, and he felt a comfort and reassurance that they would face whatever came along together. The touch was a lifeline, promising him the words that sounded deep within his soul, and he saw flickers of hope ignite within the depths of his despair.

As the sun reached higher in the sky, Alaric felt his choices weighing him down-the gravity of the past coupled with the uncertainty of his future. Taking a deep breath, the crisp air rushed into his lungs as he accepted reality: his life had been full, yet marked by darkness and regret. He gripped Lyra's hand hard in a gesture both of consolation and resolve-to cherish every moment they were together, no matter what their goodbye would be. As sun crept over the horizon and bled light upon the ground Alaric readied himself to meet what fate may throw at him-death or anything beyond, a place said to harbor change and new life. In that moment of grace, with Lyra beside him, he opted for the beauty of the present, the warmth of love they shared, and hope gleaming in the light of a new day as ready to face what awaited them together.

CHAPTER EIGHTEEN

LIGHT BEYOND THE VEIL

The air was thick with waiting as Alaric stood on the brink of change. Energy pulsed from the blood bond that bound him to Lyra, alive in the quiet of dawn. Around her neck was a pendant that started glowing brightly. The ethereal light seemed to pulse from it and connected to the remaining pieces of their blood. The very fabric of their bond was alive; waves of warmth ran through him in contrast to the cold he had suffered for centuries. The brightness shrouded itself around him, enveloping him in a promise of change and hope.

For the first time since he could not remember when, Alaric felt this strange feeling inside him—a feeling that defied the sun's deadly rays which had held him captive for so long in darkness. It ran up from the pendant, oozing through him like liquid fire as it lit the spirit. It began to dissolve whatever barriers had long confined his soul. The ancient threads of his vampirism started to break apart before him as every beat of the pendant yanked away thread after thread of his own dark past, weaving new and better for him to become.

Rather than dissolving into the sun's warm light, Alaric could feel a deep change unfolding inside of him. Energy of their bond, born of blood and love, was reshaping him from within, from his core, transforming him. The long-dead numbness to which he had grown accustomed, the freezing numbness of centuries, was gone; instead, a refreshing warmth ran through his veins and rejuvenated him in ways he never thought possible. With every beat, he felt change, a transformation that started from the powerful love that Lyra had given to him.

As the light engulfed him, his visions of the past went dancing through his mind as a film reel, in the form of a montage of memories between shadows and light. He recalled loneliness, too, that clung around him, nights lonely ones, faces of friends gone by, passing with an unremembered thought. But he balanced on either side of such thoughts, a glow of happiness within Lyra's companionship - her laughter, the warmth of her caress, sparks that caught their life within his bosom. In that moment of realization, Alaric understood the depth of their bond and realized that it was not just blood that tied them together but a love that transcended life and death.

As Alaric's body began to undergo these miraculous changes, he became acutely aware of the world around him in a way he had never experienced before. The sunlight that once torched him now felt warm and inviting, wrapping itself around him like a golden embrace. The chill in his bones, which had long been a part of him, began to melt away as a vibrant pulse of life throbbed through him with each passing moment. Each blade of grass beneath him was brought to life and felt real as, whispering through the tree, the wind sounded a melodious symphony.

Wondering, he took in his hands full of amazement by how that flesh could feel at once so strange yet also so achingly achingly familiar. From before, pale, chilly fingers of a creature from the darkness had gone; now warm, strong hands stood forth like a man drenched in hope and potentiality. He could feel the blood running through his veins, the beat of life pulsing steadily inside him—a song that indicated not only rebirth but also a purpose he never knew he needed. Alaric then realized in that moment that he was no longer a slave to his vampirism. He was becoming something far more beautiful, something that could allow him to find the light.

From a distance, Lyra gazed in wonder and saw the miraculous miracle for herself, with tears running down her cheeks as a proof of love and sacrifice that had brought about that change. She felt beyond the physical world the reverb of their bond as if it reverberated in the air. Alaric looked at her with luminous radiance; all the said with love and expression, but the glance that met their eyes conveyed complete silence. When Alaric extended his hand to hers, they grasped each other into an emblem that echoed deeply into themselves.

When the intertwined fingers touched each other, something was felt that would bond their futures together with a rope or thread. Lyra understood that it was not just a matter of Alaric's transformation; it was the climax of their partnership journey. All the difficulties and hardships they had gone through had been the elements that forged that unbreakable bond that led to this moment of transcendent beauty. The latter was a proof of how deep their love was, for it had been hard enough to survive the storm of darkness and still grew stronger.

Lyra knew that their relationship was far from being survival; their connection was growth, evolving, and a future they could look forward to as hopeful. Alaric's transformation was a celebration of everything they had fought for, a vibrant illustration of the love that had illuminated even the darkest corners of their existence.

CHAPTER NINETEEN

THE BREAK OF DAWN

As the sun continued to rise higher in the sky, the light around Alaric grew stronger, casting a warm, golden glow over the clearing.

The boundaries of his old life faded away and were replaced by the promise of a new beginning. The air was charged with energy, a tangible reminder of the power of their love. All that seemed left of vampirism tumbled apart in threads of shadow dissolving in the light. He looked into Lyra's eyes and saw the reflection of his past but bright possibilities in his future together. Lyra," he whispered, his voice shaking. "I can feel it. The darkness... it's leaving me." Words tumbled from his lips, full of wonder as it coursed through him. He could hardly grasp what was happening, but as he spoke, the warmth around him grew ever stronger, setting the truth of his transformation.

Lyra's smile was glorious, and love shone through the tears. "Yes, Alaric! You are becoming who you always meant to be," she said, her voice strong and full of unwavering belief. "This is our moment-together. You are free from the shadows."

Alaric closed his eyes again, letting himself fall under the sensations.

He found each heartbeat to beat on the pulse of earth as in a grounding force reminded of an entity he was not one anymore in this world alone. He could hear about nature awakening around them by the chirping birds and rustling leaves with some breeze carrying the scent from flowers. Every part of him spoke of life, renewal, and of love that had brought him to this moment. And now with Lyra by his side, he could fully be himself; the weight of his past turned to a source of strength, where he felt love for one another blend into the world around them, a tapestry woven into the hope, resilience, and unwavering commitment between each other.

Just when it peaked, Alaric was feeling the final dissipation of the vampire state about him like a dissipation of mist before morning sunrise. All his chill of years was obliterated with the feeling of warmth rising from within himself and set his spirit blazing for its purpose in life.

She stepped forward, her palms outlining his face as she scoured his eyes for the slightest hint of what had tormented him for so long. "Alaric, look at me," she whispered gently. "You are no longer just alive; you are living now. Today marks a new dawn, both for you and me."

The light around them intensified, and he felt rebirth under the warmth of the sun. He looked intensely at Lyra's eyes, understanding the profoundness of the love that had defined his rebirth. In every heartbeat, he knew that their tie was not just a blood connection but a journey shared in a hundred different ways over the bounds of life.

"I swear to love this life with you," he vowed, his voice dripping with conviction. "Together we'll face whatever comes our way. I'm no longer afraid."

His words had reached Lyra's heart, and, knowing it was the start of a new era, he took her heart into the clouds. Challenges she had braved and the darkness that had fallen away only made their love stronger, and they stood before a new horizon, awaiting whatever might befall.

Shared in a smile, hands intertwined, and light shining on them, they faced the rising sun. There was a different world in that place; vibrant with so much possibility. It dawned on them at that moment that love indeed makes all the difference by being the change-maker and the healer, and perhaps the light to bring some light into the darkest place.

As they stood at the precipice of that new beginning, Alaric felt a freedom he never knew.

He was free from all those shadows of his past; reborn, full of hope, passion, and a bond with a woman he had come to love. They would guide each other through this new life, facing all the joys and challenges that lay ahead with unshakeable resolve, fierce love, and everything.

Days passed, and Alaric and Lyra welcomed a new existence with open hearts and minds. They went out into the world again, rediscovering the simple pleasures of life: warmth under the sun on their skin, the laughter with friends, and the beauty that passed through every day.

Alaric revelled in the sensation of being alive, experiencing the world in vivid colors and rich textures denied him for centuries.

Lyra was the anchor for him, a guide through the complexities of mortal life while sharing some of her own discoveries with him. They went off on adventures that deepened their bond: from treks through the forest trails surrounding Oak Hollow to road trips to towns at their whim. Every moment would be filled with wonder and new memories, creating experiences that celebrated their love as they wove them together.

However, during that journey through life, he did not forget that black darkness had surrounded him a little while before. Now that he had gained that freedom from vampiric shackles, there will always be darkness waiting somewhere in the wings for their memories. This information threatened them still: though all the battles of living on the surface are there with them, this reminded Alaric and Cass of how long a distance existed between the past world in the underground world they so callously used, one day deciding to kill or love a creature and changing back.

And in the light of everything, Alaric and Lyra each felt they needed to step into the fray together in one manner. They started finding means of dealing with anything remaining of the shadows. They reached out to friends they had managed to bring aboard in the wake of their journey. There they built new relationships within bonds of friendship and common struggle. With all of these together, they faced whatever came next, which the love between them will only drive them forward better for this fight to stop shadows from their lives ever again.

In this new chapter of their lives, Alaric learned that love was not just a force that tied them together but a light to guide them through the unknown ahead. Every step they took together renewed him with a sense of purpose, commitment to protecting the life they had built and nurturing the love that had brought them together.

And so, hand in hand, Alaric and Lyra stood ready to face whatever lay beyond the threshold of their future and with that knowledge, alone, they could face any thing.

CHAPTER TWENTY

A Mortal Heart

Alaric slowly woke, the warmth of the sun filtering through the leaves above him and resting softly on his face. He blinked against the brightness, confusion muddling his mind as he adjusted to the world around him. The rustle of the forest that once had haunted memories was now singing with gentle nature sounds as it awakened. As his senses sharpened, he felt something extraordinary—a deep realization that he felt. human.

A gasp escaped his lips, and air filled his lungs, fresh and sweet, a pleasure forgotten long ago. The crisp morning air curled around him, and each inhaled breath brought back a latent spark of life. His hand pressed against his chest, feeling the rhythm beating in his heart, one he never thought he'd hear again. The beat was strong and steady and a testament to his newfound existence.

He sat up, gazing around him. The forest was brighter than ever, the colors more vivid, the sounds fuller. He could hear the birds singing, leaves rustling, and the soft flow of water nearby, all harmonizing in a symphony of life. It was as if the world had overnight become like him.

As he sat, getting used to his surroundings, he could sense a presence beside him. Lyra drew nearer to him, her eyes opened wide with a blend of wonder and relief. "He is so beautiful," he said to himself as he looked out into her, who glistened in the warm sun light of the morning like an angel. "Alaric!" she exclaimed in joy that sounded to his very soul.

Being aided by her steadying hand, he stood up again on his feet. The moment he straightened up, she wrapped her arms around him, pulling him to a tight embrace. He had longed for something like this for so long-it was different, so alive-and he had craved it for centuries. She warmed his chest with the fire that seemed to surge in her body, breathed in the comforting scent of her hair, the smell of wildflowers and sunshine. It was a feeling that reminded him that he was alive, and that he belonged.

"I can't believe it," he whispered, pulling back just enough to look into her eyes, searching for reassurance. He could see the glimmer of unshed tears, but this time they were tears of joy, a stark contrast to the sorrow that had once defined his existence.

"It's real," she whispered. "You're here, Alaric. You're alive."

Joy rose up in him, mingling with incredulity and forcing him to laugh—that feel-good yet strange sensation. The whirlwind of emotions was overwhelming, but the truth of his change anchored him.

As they stood together, Lyra helped him steady himself against a tree next to them, and they tried piecing together what had occurred. "The blood bond. it must have mingled with the magic of the heirloom," Alaric said, his voice filled with wonder. "It transformed me back into a mortal." He paused for a moment to try and process the implications of that revelation. "I'm. I'm human again.".

Lyra grinned, her eyes sparkling. "Oh, yes! Your heart is beating! You're alive, Alaric!" Her fervor unleashed a warmth in his chest that responded to the sun over their heads.

"What does it mean for us?" he asked, his heart racing at the possibilities. "What does it mean for our future?

She took another step closer to him, her eyes never leaving his face. "It means we can really be together without the shadows of your past following us. We can live, Alaric. We can explore life together as partners.".

Gratitude swept through him, a wave of gratitude for everything Lyra had given him. "I wouldn't be standing here if it weren't for you," he said, voice sincere. "Your relentless love and support. it was what brought me back. I will always be grateful for that."

"Together we'll find a way through," she said, squeezing his hand lightly. "We'll face whatever happens, just as we've always done."

As he backed off from the tree, Alaric stood with his feet upon the ground, aware at last of what that was like. He stooped to touch the blades of grass, so marvelously green, when the coolness on his skin was enough to make him shiver with pleasure. Each feeling was so easy yet marvelous in itself, each an almost magic thing now charged with the excitement of being alive.

"Come on! Let's explore!" Lyra urged, her enthusiasm infectious as she led him deeper into the forest. Alaric followed her, taking in the sights, sounds, and scents of the world around him. Every step was a revelation: an opportunity to rediscover everything he had missed during those years of darkness.

As they walked, he noticed the intricate patterns of sunlight filtering through leaves to dance across the forest floor. He could hear the gentle hum of insects and the distant sound of a stream bubbling over rocks - a reminder of the more vibrant ecosystem thriving all about them. Every detail was amplified, every breath a gist of life.

Lyra led him to a small clearing where wildflowers bloomed in riot colors. "Look at this!" she exclaimed, kneeling down to touch the petals of a bright yellow flower. "Can you believe how beautiful everything is?

Alaric knelt by her side, reaching out a hand to touch the delicate petals. "It's incredible," he breathed softly, taken aback by the brilliance of the moment. Everything seemed new-the colors brighter, scents stronger, and world more alive than he ever could have envisioned.

He drew deep in the scented air with the perfume of flowers, laughed without a weight of memories behind his pure and care-free face: "I did not know how life could feel this way," he exclaimed. "Every day's an adventure.".

And Lyra just smiled, happily. "This is only the beginning, Alaric! We have so much to see, so many things we still experience.".

They wandered throughout the morning in the forest, every new discovery a journey in itself. Alaric dipped his fingers into the cool water of the stream, marvelling at the feel as it splashed against his skin. He sat and watched as Lyra skipped stones across the surface, the ringing sound of her laughter echoing as music. The beauty of such simple joys was intoxicating, and Alaric drank them in, savoring the richness of life surrounding him.

He saw the way the sunlight settled into her hair, the look of joy that danced through her eyes. "I will never want this to end," he confessed, his heart ready to burst with love for her. "You make all things feel so. alive."

Lyra turned to him, her face softening. "And you, Alaric, you make it all worthwhile. This is our life now. We have each other and a future full of promises.".

With each passing moment they shared, Alaric found that his change was more than just skin-deep; his spirit was also awakening. There was hope, a belief that they could conquer anything the future may bring, together.

As they walked, Alaric couldn't help but feel that it was more than just a gift; it was a call. The forest, full of possibilities, held its breath, waiting for them to etch onto it their dreams. They wandered through dappled sunlit clearings, over mossy rocks, beneath the trees, and laughed through the air.

They finally reached a little rise overlooking a serene pond, its surface reflecting the blue sky above. Alaric was taken aback by the view; he felt an overwhelming urge to plunge into the cool water. "Can we swim?" he asked excitedly.

"Of course!" Lyra replied with sparkling eyes full of mischief. "I have always wanted to swim in this pond, but I never dared to.".

Not waiting for a second invitation, Alaric pulled off his shirt and ran toward the water, his heart pounding with excitement. He plunged into the cool arms of the pond, refreshing and invigorating against his skin. The feeling of being submerged, the weightlessness of his body, filled him with joy. He broke the surface, laughing and gasping for breath, the exhilaration of life surging through him.

Lyra joined him. Her laughter echoed with each splash of water as she pretended to splash him in turn. "You look funny!" she teased, grinning with glee.

"I feel great!" he hollered back at her, basking in the exuberance of the moment.

They splashed around and played in the water. The sounds of laughter went out across the clearing, but every splash and embrace seemed to celebrate the new life ahead for them as a token of the love they were developing for one another. The sun's warmth felt so warm on Alaric's face as the dancing water around him seemed joyful and free in just existing.

As the sun went down, dipping into the horizon, it cast a golden glow on the landscape. Alaric and Lyra stepped out of the pond with their bodies glistening in droplets of water. They sat down on the bank, catching their breath, the silence between them comfortable and full of unspoken promises.

"Do you think this is what it feels to be alive?" Alaric asked, his voice thoughtful. "To live each moment so vividly?"

Lyra turned to him, her expression serious yet soft. "I believe so. Life is for embracing the

joy, the pain, and all that lies in between. It's living, not existing."

The words spoke so deep within him, and he nodded, recognizing the weight of her wisdom. For too long he was confined within darkness-merely existence without any life within-until he now comprehended what it was all about-love, connection, and those little moments that fill the heart with joy.

Alaric knew it was going to start at that very moment. They could now establish a future of love and light; they could discover the world beside each other as partners, free from his shadows past.

As the sunset over the horizon painted the orange and pink hues of the sky, Alaric had all these feelings of gratitude and love towards Lyra. "Thanks for believing in me, for never giving up. You gave me a second chance at life."

Lyra smiled, with unshed tears overflowing from her eyes. "And thanks for taking that chance with me. Together, we can face anything.".

With the sun setting and the twinkling starts above, Alaric felt Lyra's warmth as they took this step together- two souls brought together in love, yet now much more than that. He was an explorer of limitless possibilities, now with a purpose to face everything that awaits them with boldness and hope.

Under the vastness of the night sky, in the midst of the forest, Alaric and Lyra embraced the promise of the future knowing that together they could create an eternity full of love, laughter, and endless adventures.

CHAPTER TWENTY-ONE

NEW HORIZONS

The decision to leave Oak Hollow could be felt as bittersweet for Alaric during the morning sun, while bathing in warm golden light which shone on the woods where they had taken cover so long. Alaric stood there at the very edge of their temporary abode, and his heart went swirling like a whirlpool, with this mixed feeling:. Together, he and Lyra started to pack their belongings, full of memories of a life lived in the shadows and dreams woven under the stars.

While folding clothes and collecting some meager possessions, Alaric couldn't help sneaking glances at the towering trees that had watched over his transformation. The other side of the forest he found was a prison where his dark past held over him, while it stood like a sanctuary to him wherein all the beauty that Lyra presented comforted him with serenity. He felt sad while leaving behind the whispers from the woods, the sounds of rustling leaves under breezy winds, and haunted night songs.

Now Lyra paused beside him when she noticed him to be so deep in thought and touched her hand on the side of his shoulder lightly. "It is okay that you are feeling sad; this place is part of you journey, after all." She continued. "Some piece of this will travel with us for good".

Alaric nodded, his chest swelling with gratitude. "I will always hold dear the nights we spent here," he said in a voice thick with emotion. "Every moment spent under the stars has shaped me into who I am now.".

They kept up the moment of silence and allowed memories to just flood them: the first meeting in the misty forest, the secrets shared in moonlight, the thrill of discovery as they explored their feelings with each other. Those memories were now treasures etched into their hearts, and when they left Oak Hollow, it would carry its spirit.

As they stuffed the last of their belongings into the car, Alaric turned back to the forest one last time. A silent promise was forming in his mind: he would embrace his humanity fully, letting the light of this new life illuminate his path.

The car roared to life, and as they pulled away from Oak Hollow, Alaric felt a rush of freedom, exhilarating. The road before them curled through the rolling hills and verdant landscape, with each mile stretching them farther away from the shadows that haunted their past. They rolled down their windows to let the warm breeze toss their hair around, the scents of fresh grass and wildflowers filled their lungs with the smell of life.

Their journey comprised quaint little towns and great cities, where every stop took them through glimpses into a world Alaric never knew. He enjoyed street food at their local places, indulging in all sorts of dishes like homemade pie to the ones dancing around flavors. Alaric enjoyed simple meal times with Lyra as bubbles of laughter brewed between them as they bantered which dessert they would have first.

"Okay, how about this?" Lyra said with a glint of mischief in her eyes. "We order one of everything and see who can finish it all!"

Alaric laughed at that. The sound boomed through the cozy café they had discovered. "You're on! But I'm warning you—I've got a vampire's appetite!"

There were many impromptu adventures en route for their road trip. One afternoon, there was a magnificent viewpoint over the valley looking so beautiful that nothing short of words could attempt to describe it completely. It was a stretched view and the rolling green hills along with golden hills went out into endless sight. Alaric breathed deeply, casting away all the burdens from his world, with Lyra by his side and beneath warming sunbeams.

Let's take a picture," she said, taking out her phone. They posed silly, arms stretching outward, smiles wide, snapping pictures that would capture pure moment joy. When the camera snapped, Alaric felt he had reached quite far. This was now his life—laughter, love, and new promise.

As they rode over miles, Alaric felt that he has broken the chains of the past. It was intoxicating to be able to wander the world hand in hand with Lyra. They danced through a great city, spinning in neon light as the sound of music washed over them. They strolled through street markets hand in hand, eating candies and talking with kind vendors as they steeped themselves in the vibrant tapestry that surrounded them.

As they continued their journey, the conversations between Alaric and Lyra deepened as they transitioned from banter to serious discussion over their aspirations. On one evening, after having had their sunset picnic atop a hill, they lie flat on a blanket as every star in the sky made its way one by one into the twilight sky.

I always wanted to be an astronomer, Lyra said, gazing up into the heavens. Stargazing has always been my escape, my way of understanding the universe. I want to discover new worlds and share that knowledge with others.

Turning to her, Alaric's chest swelled with pride. "You would be great at that," he said with conviction. "Your passion is contagious. I can already envision you speaking to a crowd, telling of your findings."

Her cheeks flushed warmly as she smiled. "And you? Now that you are human, what will you do?

Alaric nodded, lost in thought over the question. "I want everything I never had. Love, friendship, adventure... I want to live the simple pleasure of life. I want to find meaning in my existence, make every moment precious."

Lyra nodded in understanding. Glimmering in her eyes is the spark of comprehension. "We can help each other pursue our dreams. I will share my knowledge of stargazing with you, and you can teach me about fearless living.".

This filled Alaric with hope because they were partners in every way meant to take on the world together. He knew a sense of belonging that he had never known before: knowing that they could build a life filled with love, understanding, and shared aspirations.

But as he walked, Alaric discovered that the road ahead of him was not without its troubles. For all the joys his transformation brought him, shadows still loomed from his old self. Sometimes, he could feel the insecurities crawling under his skin, carrying with them the weight of all the mistakes he had ever made.

One evening, after a really tough day, Alaric sat on the edge of their hotel bed, staring blankly at the wall. Lyra sensed his turmoil and approached him, concern etched on her face. "What's wrong?" she asked softly, her hand resting on his back.

"I just... I cannot shake this feeling of inadequacy," he said, his voice heavy with vulnerability. "I've made so many mistakes in my past. What if I mess this up too? What if I'm not deserving of this second chance?"

Lyra knelt beside him, never drawing her eyes away. "You are worthy, Alaric. You fought so hard to become the man you are today. We all have a past, but it does not define us. It is what we do going forward that matters."

Her words hit a chord within him, though doubt still lingered there. "But what if I fail? What if I am not strong enough to handle this new life?

She took in a deep breath and turned with a serious expression saying, "You are never alone in this. We'll face the challenges together. You're strong enough to confront everything that comes your way. I believe in you.".

Her unwavering support wrapped him in a warm embrace, and Alaric felt the weight slowly begin to shift. "Thank you, Lyra," he said, "I don't know what I would do without you.".

They were the face of each other, gradually going through the issues collectively. Alaric taught his lessons on Lyra, as well as gave space to her to be that one anchor when he himself became haunted by his past experiences. They stood in front of those problems, moving ahead together, handling their array of fears and doubts up-front.

They once met a group of locals in one small town that doubted Alaric's past. Alaric felt the judgment as whispers accompanied him down the streets. Memories of his former life flashed before his eyes as he continued to walk straight, his head held high due to Lyra.

Just remember, you are not defined by what you once were, Lyra whispered softly as they walked, her hand intertwined with his. "You are forging a new path, and I'm proud of you for it.".

She came as a torch of belief that showed him into the rest of his dark past and kept him looking at them, not looking away from them. Gradually, every obstacle, Alaric found human in himself. Imperfection and strife alone bring meaning into life and give it depth, richness.

Through it all, Alaric and Lyra discovered the truth of their love. It wasn't just about the happy times; it was about facing the hard times together, growing closer with each obstacle they overcame. They learned to communicate openly, sharing their fears and triumphs, knowing that vulnerability only strengthened their bond.

As they continued their drive, Alaric got clearer. The struggles had not been a sign of weakness but rather opportunities to improve. Each challenge would teach him resilience, and with Lyra by his side, he began embracing the idea of truly living life.

They parked one evening at a panoramic turnout, sitting on the car hood as the stars were twinkling above. Alaric gazed out toward the endless expanse of the universe, felt something deep in his soul as the world was connected to everything, to himself. "Remember our first night in Oak Hollow?" he asked almost in a whisper.

Lyra nodded, a soft smile breaking across her face. "I recall how fascinated I was about the stars and how far away you seemed. But now... She turned her gaze to him and was looking at him like there was dancing starlight inside her. "Now you're living, breathing, thriving-with me. It's magic."

"Yeah," Alaric said, his heart swelling with affection. "I never thought I could feel this way again. Thanks for helping me see beauty in life."

Under the stars, Alaric realized this trip was about so much more than a drive: it became a celebration of life and love. They were not running away from the past, embracing the horizons, ready to make something that filled life with endless possibilities.

Every passing day made Alaric return to himself. He had put shadows of his past life behind, and he was full of hope for what the days ahead would bring. In hand in hand with Lyra, they forged on a new path to face head-on whatever lay before them with courage and love.

And so, under the big vast sky full of stars, Alaric and Lyra took their first steps into a new chapter in life-one filled with adventure, discovery, and the promise of a brighter future.

RUINS AND REVELATIONS

Alaric and Lyra found themselves driving to places that ended in being some of the oldest ancient vampire sites with a great deal of history and magic attached to them. With every place they visited, Alaric's door was flung open into the past, giving him an opportunity to learn secrets which created his being. He and Lyra strolled across the broken castles, where stones whispered tales of time that had long since gone, and they searched through sacred places where rituals in blood and power bound vampires together.

As they approached the first destination-an old castle standing on top of a hill, Alaric felt the strange pull towards its weathered walls. Structure standing like a sentinel from yesteryears with towers reaching toward the sky, he could feel the connection almost palpable. The air was full of the weight of history, and every stone vibrated with the echoes of those who had come before him.

"What do you feel?" Lyra asked, her voice soft against the rustling leaves surrounding them.

"I don't know how to explain it," Alaric said, his eyes scanning the facade of the castle. "It's as if the place remembers me. It's haunting and beautiful at the same time."

They stepped through the arched entrance of the castle and the cool air enclosed them like a shroud. Inside, the faint light lit up the leftovers of grand halls and old tapestries-remnants of life lived centuries ago. Alaric ran his fingers along the walls, feeling the grooves and imperfections of each one, every one a story in itself.

Do you think this is one of your ancestors' homes?" Lyra wondered, her eyes wide with wonder, drinking in the ancient architecture.

"It's possible," Alaric said, a shiver of recognition coursing through him. "I have always felt a connection to the past, as if there are parts of me that belonged here long before I ever existed.".

As they wandered through the castle, they came upon a room hidden behind a large, imposing wooden door. Rummaging around the space, it's strewn about is left: dead candles, shards of glass, and crumbling scrolls. Alaric felt an energy surge as he entered, however, the air buzzing with power from both the machinations of magic with his own prana.

Look at this, said Lyra, holding up one of the scrolls, with its parchment brittle with age, "It speaks of blood bonds and ancient rituals."

Alaric came closer and began to read over her shoulder; the scroll was full of details about blood bonds among the vampires, which could become stronger or be broken with powerful rituals. He tied a knot in his chest as he realized how well this applied to their own bond.

"It says here that true love can transcend even the darkest of curses," he whispered, his heart pounding. "We were destined to find each other."

Lyra gazed up at him with her sparkling eyes. "This bond we share... it's not just a coincidence. It's a part of something greater, something that has existed for centuries."

As they traveled through places, the story of Alaric's history came alive as if pages from a long-forgotten book. They came to old ruins, where the whispers of old vampires who lived long before were hovering in the air, sharing stories of love and loss and sacrifice. And with each place, memories were echoing - memories of the night that was dominated by magic when vampires lived under ancient codes and secrets.

With every location, Alaric learned more about the blood bond that had changed him. He found out it was an extremely rare bond, formed from the fires of love and sacrifice. Scrolls and artifacts said that ancient rituals could even strengthen a bond or snap it apart altogether, exposing the fine balance between love and darkness.

Standing there amidst the remains of an ancient chapel, Alaric felt his heart pound with associations of his past. "These places... they've seen so much. The stories they could tell," he said with a thick voice. "I never knew the depth of my line until now.".

"You are no longer a vampire, Alaric," Lyra said as she turned toward him. "You have human in you, and it only makes your story so much stronger.".

In that moment, Alaric realized it was not a mere accident of destiny; it was a fruit of love and sacrifice which he and Lyra shared. The blood bond, he realized, proved how strong they were; love can prevail even over the darkest curses.

There in the midst of that destruction, amidst the wreckage of what might well have been a lost world, Alaric and Lyra found sanctuary in love. They sat upon the steps of the ancient chapel, there watching as sunset approached its golden hue upon the stones of that place.

"We've beaten the odds," Lyra whispered softly. "Your transformation, our journey... it's all a testament to what we can overcome together."

Alaric nodded, his heart filling with gratitude. "I used to think love was a curse—a weakness. But now I see it as our greatest strength. It's what has brought me back to life."

They were speaking intimately of the struggles that they were facing, right from the dangerous uncertainty of their early days in relationship to vulnerable moments that had strengthened them. Each memory was like a thread sewn into the tapestry of love and was colored with depth and richness.

"Do you remember that night we were gazing at the stars, stargazing in Oak Hollow?" Alaric asked, a grin dancing on his lips. "How we talked about dreams under the stars?"

The smile lit up Lyra's face. "Oh, I do! It's like the universe was actually listening to us, taking us toward our destinies.

Those dreams are becoming our reality, Alaric replied, taking her hands in his. "I can only wait to see what the future holds for us.".

They kissed softly, as if their lips were only gently brushing against each other in a promise of what was going to be. They knew at that moment that their love was not just a force that brought them together but a catalyst for change, a beacon of hope that lit even the darkest corners of their hearts.

As they sat amidst the ruins, watching the last rays of sunlight fade into twilight, Alaric felt this overwhelming sense of possibility. Their journey was far from over; it was only the beginning of a new chapter filled with adventures yet to come.

With the horizon unfolding before them, Alaric and Lyra rediscovered their purpose in the world. They stood, hand in hand, at the setting sun as orange and pink hues spread all over the sky. In this world, anything felt possible, and each second was a chance to love the life they had worked hard to achieve.

"Promise me something," Lyra said, turning to him, her expression serious.

"Anything," Alaric replied, his heart racing at the intensity of her gaze.

"Promise me that we'll keep on exploring, that we'll keep seeking out new adventures together. No matter what challenges come our way, we'll face them together."

"I promise," Alaric said, his voice steady. "We will embrace every moment, every challenge, together."

They kissed again as the sun went below the horizon, their hearts entwined in a kiss ready for whatever tomorrow may bring. And with each beat, Alaric felt the strength of that connection - a bond that was unbreakable and forged in love and resilience.

As darkness filled the landscape, Alaric looked into Lyra's eyes and felt hope spill over. "I never thought I could feel like this again," he said with a deep emotion in his voice. "You gave me a second chance in life."

Lyra smiled as her eyes reflected the starlight above them. "And you showed me what love is. We can conquer anything together.".

Thus they lift their eyes towards the skies, with their souls flowing with dreams and aspirations. The two were going to take over the world, side by side, as they stepped out into an uncertain future. Each passing day becomes an adventure, a penning of history, the adventure of stepping into a remnant of history creating love, laughter, and many possibilities ahead.

And so, with the night sky as their witness, Alaric and Lyra embarked on their next chapter, one filled with hope, healing, and the promise of a love that would last through the ages.

CHAPTER TWENTY-THREE

HOMECOMING

With Alaric and Lyra driving down the well-known roads of Oak Hollow, the past swept over them and blended with the heavy air of fear. The country rolled out before them, tapestry-like, trees so dense and leafy as to almost hide the view of others sparse and wild and brown, and hill followed after hill in curves so perfect that the memories of every turn of the road came up like spirits from the past. Alaric felt mixed emotions of excitement and nervousness as they approached the town of the starting point of their journey; a place that, at one time, held dark shades for him. The aroma of pine and earthy smell filled up the car, bringing forth the echo of laughter and whispers exchanged beneath starlit skies. He recalled the day when, in that enigmatic misty glade, he first laid eyes on Lyra and the encounter that was to change his life forever. With each mile gone by, he felt it to be one more chapter in a tale so long scripted that was sullied by shadows but promised now the illumination of a new dawn.

With much pageantry, Alaric walked out of the car his heart hammering, towards what awaited him in that clearing-the leaves rustling with a gentle breeze for trees higher than he ever remembered-illuminating and lightening up the skies. Over by his side emerged Lyra, slid hand in to his, the both stepping across towards where life paths joined for the first time. In the steps, the weight he had carried began to set free, replaced by feelings of belonging that surged into him. The clearing of fear and isolation now radiates with warmth and possibility in it. Together, moving closer to the very same spot where they had shared stories for the first time around, the constellations twinkling above them in the form of ancient, watchful guardians over reunion.

Standing in that clearing, Alaric thought to himself how much he'd travelled since that night. From being a creature of the night, haunted and lonely, drifting through centuries for no purpose, to be standing here next to Lyra and feeling the absolute gratitude pouring over him. For a moment, the sun shining upon his skin and the rustling of the leaves and the laughter ringing in the air reminded him that he was indeed alive—truly alive. It was a realization that the darkness that once shrouded him was pierced by the light of love and hope. He turned to Lyra whose eyes sparkled with glee and they stood in the beauty around them for one moment, savoring the transformation of this hallowed space.

Without premeditation, Alaric suggested that they develop a small ritual for this homecoming. He picked up a smooth stone. The surface was cool beneath his touch. He cut a heart onto it, for this represented the union that was sprouting within them from their hardships. Lyra grinned as her heart filled to the brim with tenderness. She picked another rock, slightly smaller but similarly rounded and flattened, then etched another symbol upon it-a star, indicating the aspirations of her soul. They positioned stones at the base of the tree in the same near site, marking their distances crossed over and the love sprouting here in this consecrated place. Simple action but meaningful because it depicted that they would show honor about what had been transpiring while moving to embrace further.

"This feels right," Lyra whispered softly, her eyes glued to the stones at the base of the tree. "It's like we're grounding our love in this place, ensuring that it's part of Oak Hollow forever."

Alaric nodded, his heart swelling with warmth. "Every time we come back here, we'll remember what we've built together. This place will always hold our story."

Alaric knew a strange sense of peace set upon him as they both stood within the clearing. This clearing no longer represented darkness in any capacity but instead loved, and transformed into newfound life; and if there was more to this strange life beyond this place now that she was at his side to share it, it would, in itself be fine regardless of what's to follow. And, together then, they drank deep with the crisp smell of that fresh air teeming through the very atmosphere, laden with the lifeblood nature, home smell. This was their sanctuary, where their love had grown and flourished, and now they were ready to nurture it further.

They walked through those familiar woods, discovering everything about each other and all the first times. Seemed as if every step of the way opened up the floodgates of memories-whispers shared secrets, promises made in the light of stars, and the silence of their laughter in quiet woods.

Alaric pointed to the exact spot where they had stargazed on their very first night, and his heart just welled as he thought about the excitement of the stars that night.

"Do you remember that night?" he said, chuckling. "You were sure you'd seen a shooting star and we made a wish."

Lyra laughed, the sparkle in her eyes full of mischief. "I still believe it was a sign. Look where we are now!"

"That night changed everything," Alaric replied, his tone serious now. "It was the beginning of my journey back to life."

And the light that she shed upon him was a beauty to behold, Lyra thought, when Alaric looked up at her, his face softening into a warmth. "You gave me so much, Alaric," she said, her voice filled with a gratitude. "You taught me that love could shine through darkness. I will always be in your debt for that."

He entwined his fingers with hers, walking. "And I will always love you for bringing light to my existence. You've changed me in ways that I never even thought was possible.".

They continued exploring, where hidden nooks and familiar paths both felt strange and yet intimate. Sunlight, filtering through the leaves of the trees, cast their warm glow upon the ascent of a small hill into the valley. The landscape that unfolded before them was such a breathtaking view of the rolling hills and valleys shining in the golden light of dusk.

"This is lovely," Lyra breathed, taking in the vista. "It feels as if the world is spreading open before us."

"Yes," Alaric concurred, feeling the crushing weight of his past pressing down upon him as new hope for a future bloomed in his chest. "There is so much we have in front of us."

They spread out across the grass at dusk on a blanket, sharing tales of travel and dreams for what was to come. Alaric felt an emotion wash over him that brought him deep contentment in the twinkling stars that began to appear above as Lyra laughed. He knew at once that the darkness no longer held them captive in bondage.

"Do you ever think about what's ahead of us?" Lyra asked, her voice curious.

"All the time," he admitted. "I want to experience everything—travel, love, build a life together. I want to be there for you as you chase your dreams."

Lyra smiled and her eyes sparkled with light. "And I want to support you too, whatever you choose to do. You have so much to offer the world, Alaric."

He leaned forward, captivated by her candor. "I want to help others, maybe share my story. If I can help even one see that change is possible, that love heals, then it's all worthwhile.".

Your path is inspiring," Lyra said, her voice filled with conviction. "You have a gift, Alaric. You have seen both sides of the coin, and that can be helpful to others in their search.".

They articulated their hopes and dreams and their fears against the background of twinkling stars. Each word exchanged seemed to add to the depth of their connection. They were more than two souls tied together; they were partners promising the future.

As the night got darker, a chill from the cold air of the evening set in. They clung to each other, warmth seeming to seek each other in their embrace. Alaric felt something he never knew before: finally home.

"Promise me one thing," he said, breaking the comfortable silence. "Promise me we'll always find our way back to this clearing, no matter where life takes us."

Lyra nodded, her face solemn. "I promise. This will always be our sanctuary—a place where we can reconnect and remember who we are."

"Together," Alaric added firmly.

"Together," she repeated, sealing their promise with a soft kiss, the warmth of whose lips set within him a flame of hope.

As they looked up to the stars, Alaric sensed a peace over them—the feeling that they are in exactly the right place. Oak Hollow, that used to be a shadow-filled place, was transformed into a haven of light as their journey and the love that led them back were represented by this gesture.

With Lyra sitting by his side, he knew that they could get through everything that came along. His dark past shadow no longer weighed him down; it was inside, molding him into the full-of-love, full-of-hope, better-tomorrow person who stood before him. Through the dark waters of his life, they went hand in hand, into the unknown sea of their lives.

And as they drifted into night, embracing one another, Alaric knew he finally found home – a place filled with love, laughter, and endless possibilities. Home had never felt so right.

CHAPTER TWENTY-FOUR

Under Familiar Stars

The night had fallen over Oak Hollow, and the stars came out like diamonds in a velvet sky, making the world look painted with twinkling lights. Alaric and Lyra laid a blanket in the clearing, feeling the cool earth beneath them. Lying back to gaze at the stars, Alaric felt a deep sense of peace wash over him. He thought of how the stars seemed different now. The twinkling constellations up in the sky told ancient stories and stories of love which had weathered time and the universe was not empty after all.

Lyra looked up at Alaric, and her eyes lit up as she drew the shape of a constellation. "Look there, Orion!" she called out, pointing up toward the sky. "I always loved how he watched over the night.".

Alaric followed where her eyes were directed, his smile broadening. "And there's his belt," he said, identifying the three bright stars that lay in a straight line. "I remember you telling me about the myth of Orion and how he was such a fearless hunter.".

Lyra was so enthusiastic as she narrated the tale with the addition of details related to the constellations and their importance. Speaking with her reminded Alaric of the nights and nights they had spent sharing tales and dreams, with which he cherished those nights so much. He who used to be a lone wanderer in the darkness now basked in Lyra's light.

In the dead quiet of night, they begin telling stories for each other about what was happening from the last place they set foot here on. Lyra went bright with enthusiastic words and speeches about how thrillingly traveling was going for them-in awe about the wonderful breathtaking landscapes which they visited. She discussed the fabulous fascinations through people she meets along their journey. However, for every moment together, that experience brought more into this tapestry by the making and growth through a shared story.

Do you recall the mountains? she laughed with the bubbles in her voice. We thought we were going to hike to the top, but that was one steeper trail than we had anticipated!

Alaric laughed, shaking his head. "I remember you insisting we could conquer it. And then, when we finally made it to the top, I could see the pride in your eyes, even as we both collapsed in exhaustion!"

"And the view!" Lyra added, her voice growing soft with nostalgia. "It was worth every step. I had never felt so alive. It was like standing on top of the world.".

Alaric listened intently as she recounted their adventures, his heart swelling with pride and love. With every laugh and every tear they had shared, they had brought themselves closer to the love they now cherished. He felt fortunate to have walked alongside her, knowing that they had created something beautiful together—a bond that transcended the trials they had faced.

The stars shone above, and the couple reminisced about how love had really changed them both into creatures they would never have conceived of in a lifetime of imagination. Lyra found herself gaining strength and building confidence from the examples shown by Alaric - his valor in accepting human nature - but it went beyond mere physical changes that she witnessed; it showed emotional maturity, as she saw how he began trusting and opening up his heart after all the time he was alone.

"I never thought I was capable of loving someone like this," she said honestly, her voice steady despite the vulnerability. "It's okay to be that vulnerable, to let the right person in. Thank you for helping me discover who I am."

Alaric turned to her, his gaze unwavering. "And I've learned to hope again. You brought light into my world when I thought it was lost forever. You taught me that love is worth the risk, that it can change everything."

He took his time to see the seriousness of their affair, the surge of joy he was having in travelling with her. The love had worked as a transformative factor changing them, forcing them beyond their thought. He even felt how their shared burden was creating an attachment so that both could grow more than their thought and this unique understanding had become them.

He lies under the vast night sky, feeling part of something greater than himself. Every twinkling star he sees reminds him of beauty in existence and of fates intertwined. His realization was that their love would be part of the tapestry of the universe, as woven into the fabric of time and space. A beautiful realization that cut above the boundaries of his or her life; the two were timeless and infinite.

"I consider all the constellations," Alaric murmured, tracing the silhouette of Lyra's hand with his fingers. "Each star symbolizes a story, a life experienced. It humbles you to think how big it is and connected everything really is."

Lyra nodded, her eyes shining through with starlight. "It's as if all our moments are stars that shine in our constellation: the struggles, the joys, the love-all intertwining us like we're part of something predestined."

Turning towards her, he felt filled with gratitude in his heart. "I want to forever cultivate this bond, Lyra. No matter what life has in store for us, I want it to be the beacon light that guides our love through it all."

She squeezed his hand warmly and smiled. "And I do too. Whatever happens, we face it together, as a team. We have come so far, and I believe we can face anything that comes our way.

In all the gazing at stars, night deepened around them. Alaric felt hope soar. He reached for Lyra's hand and wrapped his fingers around hers, drawing her into a world held suspended in time. And in the quiet of the clearing they shared dreams and aspirations and their voices intermixed with the soft rustling of leaves and the far hooting of an owl.

What do you dream of for us?" Alaric asked, his voice as low as a whisper so it wouldn't disturb the magic of the moment.

"I dream of building a home together, a place to feel safe and free. I want a garden filled with flowers, a space in which we can make memories and share our lives.".

Alaric's heart skipped a beat at her idea. "I love that idea. And I want a cozy nook filled with books, where we can curl up together and lose ourselves in stories."

"Exactly!" Lyra exclaimed, her excitement contagious. "And I imagine us having friends over, laughter echoing in our home, filled with warmth and love.".

A smiling picture of their future, a life in tandem - he smiled at the way she painted it. "Just sounds perfect, Lyra. Full of love, laughter, and adventure,"

"But certainly it will not be an easy life,"

she warned, a seriousness creeping into her voice as she continued, "but I believe we'll manage. Together.".

Alaric nodded, a determination settling over him. "No matter what life throws our way, we'll face it as a team. We are stronger together, and love will guide us through."

As the night drew into the cold darkness of evening, they drew together to each other, seeking the warm comfort of one another's arms. Alaric felt a sense of belonging he had never known before or realized existed for him-a sense that he finally had come home.

Promise me one thing, he said, breaking the comfortable silence. Promise me we'll always find our way back to this clearing no matter where life takes us.

Lyra gazed long into his eyes. Sincere, her response was. "I promise. This will always be a sanctuary for us—whenever we need to rediscover ourselves and get hold of who we really are."

"Us, I added, my voice definite.

Together, she repeated, sealing their vow with a soft kiss, the glow of her lips igniting a spark of hope within him.

With the twinkling of stars above, Alaric knew their love story was only in its starting phase. They would have to face their challenges and navigate through those paths as they chased after their dreams. But he was more than ready for it. Every moment they spent together under the stars would strengthen the bond between them, a reminder that they were two souls drifting across the vast expanse of the universe, but most importantly, partners in love and in purpose.

As they slept off into the night curled up in each other's arms, Alaric realized that he had finally found his place in the world, and it was one filled with love, laughter, and endless possibilities. The vast sky above them felt like a promise, like an unstretched canvas waiting for them to paint their story, step by step, hand in hand, under the familiar stars that had witnessed the beginning of their journey.

CHAPTER TWENTY-FIVE

Dreams Among the Constellations

The next morning, the sun rose over Oak Hollow and Lyra slept in refreshed with renewed resolve. Soft golden rays streamed through the window casting warm rays across the room. She was still wrapped in the afterglow of what she had found out the night before like the afterglow of stars that lingered in her head. She was called to the astronomy profession through her journey and inspiration about the universe. Her shared dreams with Alaric sounded like cosmic alignments leading her toward a path that sounded good to her heart. She envisioned herself studying heavenly bodies, trying to figure out the mysteries of space, and teaching science literacy to others, all inspired to do so just as Alaric had inspired her to do. The possibility of unraveling the secrets of stars, of investigating the universe's mysteries, sparked fire in her.

As she gets up and dressed, there is an air of numerous possibilities buzzing through her brain. She envisioned sitting at a laboratory table covered by telescopes and star charts, churning out tons of research papers for other folks to gain knowledge from, showing them just how wide and amazing space could be. This idea excited her of how she was to be presenting before the classroom to express her interest in astronomy for the younger generation of pupils who eagerly listened and learnt. That is not only a dream; that's a call for action-a call to action, in this case-and one to which she has promised herself not to look back.

The air was filled with the aroma of freshly brewed coffee and freshly baked pastries as she joined Alaric in the kitchen. Breakfast had been prepared so lovingly, just like every detail of their life. The sun shone brightly to caress them as they sat at the table. Lyra felt her heart beating faster as she looked forward to telling the man who had become her greatest supporter about her dream.

"Alaric," she started, her voice a little shaky with excitement. "I want to be an astronomer. I want to understand the stars that guided us and teach it to others." Each word out of her mouth spoke volumes about her newly found purpose, her eyes sparkling like diamonds.

Alaric's eyes softened, and he leaned forward, his face filled with encouragement. "That sounds fantastic, Lyra. You've always had this connection to the stars. I can really see how much this means to you." His heart swelled with admiration for her determination and vision. He always thought that she could make this journey and succeeded, but now he felt excitement that saw her in the light of pursuing it further.

"Really?" she asked; her voice was barely louder than a whisper, and vulnerabilities were etched on the face.

"Absolutely," Alaric replied, making his features light up. "You deserve to chase the dream. I will walk with you every step along the way."

As they continued their breakfast, Lyra felt the weight of uncertainty lift from her shoulders. The more they spoke about her aspirations, the clearer her path became. They discussed the possibility of Lyra attending university, exploring programs in astronomy and astrophysics. Alaric offered to help her with applications, knowing how much this dream meant to her.

"What schools do I look at?" she asks, her mind racing off with possibilities. "I want to find the perfect fit, but there's just so many options."

Alaric pulls out his phone and starts researching on it. "Let's find some of the best programs in the country. Let's look for universities with great astronomy departments, possibly even some with access to good observatories."

Lyra's eyes went wide with excitement. "Oh, that would be amazing! And what about scholarships? I want to make sure I can afford it."

Alaric nodded, fully engaged. "I'll help you search for scholarships and grants. We'll make this happen, Lyra.".

They kept talking, one idea flowing into another. Alaric proposed that they travel to observatories around the world, witness meteor showers, and attend lectures together. "I want to be by your side for every moment of your journey," he declared, knowing that their relationship was a partnership built on mutual dreams and aspirations.

"I love that idea," Lyra said, her heart racing. "We could even plan a trip to a dark sky reserve where we can see the Milky Way without light pollution!"

"Exactly! Think of the stories we can share and the experiences we'll have. This is just the beginning for us," he said, his voice brimming with enthusiasm.

As they shared their visions, the air around them pulsed with excitement. Each was a stepping stone toward future adventures, knowledge, and love. They spoke of the night sky at national parks and remote islands where cities did not light up those dark skies.

"Imagine lying on the beach, the waves crashing, and the stars above us," Lyra said, her eyes shining with wonder. "We could bring a telescope and spend the whole night just observing."

Alaric laughed, "I'll bring the hot cocoa, and you can guide me through the constellations."

Lyra nodded, a dreamy smile gracing her lips. "It's a date."

In a beautiful moment, they promised themselves that they would always support their dreams, no matter what size or shape they had. Lyra took the hands of Alaric and reminded him that they were the strength of his love. "No matter where we go or whatever we face, we will be there for each other, always," she said.

Alaric held her hands tight and could feel the weight of the words. "Always," he promised, his heart swelling with love. And they kissed, sealing that commitment to each other and a bright future ahead. Hope filled the air as if promise was all their love was going to lead them into the adventures waiting.

As they finished their breakfast, a hint of excitement still clings to the air. They longed to start this new part of their lives together. With dreams and aspirations apparently as vast as the stars, Alaric and Lyra were now to explore this vastness and mystery of the universe in order to unearth them—all because they had each other, and hand in hand, they would be running into the future.

Let's go for a walk," Alaric suggested after breakfast, wanting to soak in the beauty of Oak Hollow. They strolled hand in hand through the familiar streets, the sun casting long shadows on the ground as they moved toward the outskirts of town.

Lyra pointed out familiar sights, her voice animated with each one, and memories pouring in about it. "That is the old oak where I used to read there, and there is a bookstore where I first met that book on astronomy. I just fell in love," she reminisced.

Alaric laughed when he said, "Remember that book? You spoke about it for weeks after.".

They laughed, and the sound carried out across the crisp morning air. It was good to remember, to anchor themselves in the love they'd made and the future they were carving out together.

Lyra stopped at a small hill overlooking Oak Hollow, taking in the view. "This place has so many memories," she said softly. "But I think I'm ready for new ones.".

Alaric stood beside her, gazing out at the town she once thought to be too confining. "Me too," he said with a sense of resolve. "We will live a life of adventure and discovery. The world is ours for the taking.

Returning home, they sat at the dining table, excitedly piling papers upon papers. It was covered with all their notes regarding universities, scholarships, and travel plans. "We need to create a timeline," Alaric said. "When would you like to start applying to schools?

"Now that I can start making those plans, I think I'd like to begin this fall," Lyra responded. "I want to get settled into a routine before classes start. I'll also need time before any entrance exams."

Alaric nodded vigorously, taking some notes down. "And we'll start looking for local observatories for volunteer work. First-hand experience is what would help you add to the resume."

Fantastic! I can start to connect with local astronomers and attend public lectures. It is going to be an awesome way to get in contact with people in the field".

They spent hours debating their options, filling the room with laughter and enthusiasm. Afternoon slipped by as they steeped in possibilities, tossed about ideas and visions of a future both shiny and bright.

They stepped out as the sun set down outside when the evening started. It painted the sky with a warm orange and pink tinge. They sat there on the porch steps in each other's arms. They just enjoyed the moment they were in.

"See the sky," Alaric said, pointing across the horizon. "Be able to imagine how it will look tonight?"

Lyra smiled, resting her head against his shoulder. "I can't wait to see the stars again. It feels like they're calling us."

"Let's make a plan to go stargazing tonight," Alaric suggested. "We can take the blanket to our clearing and just lie there, like we did before."

"Perfect," Lyra agreed, her heart fluttering with anticipation. "I want to share all the constellations I've learned about."

Later that evening, they readied snacks and a telescope. Excitement had started to bubble up, and they walked into the clearing. The air was cool and crisp, but familiar surroundings enveloped them into comfort. Tall trees towered above them, whispering secrets in the breeze.

They spread the blanket on the grass. When they settled down, Lyra couldn't

help but glance up at the darkening sky. One by one, stars began to appear, twinkling like diamonds scattered across black velvet.

"Look!" she exclaimed, pointing at the first visible star. "That's Vega. It's one of the brightest stars in the night sky."

Alaric marveled at her enthusiasm. "You've really been studying, haven't you?"

"I do," she said, her voice bursting with enthusiasm. "I want to be able to share all of this with others, just as you pushed me to do."

They spent hours curled up in each other's arms, sharing stories, laughter, and dreams while gazing at the stars. Each constellation Lyra pointed out felt like a promise of the adventures yet to come.

"See that one? That's Cassiopeia, the Queen. She is said to represent beauty and resilience," she explained.

Alaric listened carefully, feeling his heart swelling with pride. "You are so beautiful, Lyra. You embody that spirit."

Lyra blushed her cheeks warm as she looked at him with a sweet smile. "And you are my constant star, Alaric. I would not be here without you."

The night wore on, and each sank into silent thought. Lyra's mind ran with the possibilities, the future full of hope and promise. She envisioned standing on a podium at a university, sharing her passion for the stars with eager students.

And as she looked up at the stars, she felt a wave of gratitude. She was no longer that girl in that small town, yearning for something more. With Alaric by her side, she felt she could reach for the stars.

"Promise me something," she said suddenly, turning to him, her eyes so earnest. "No matter where this journey takes us, we'll never lose the dreams. We'll never stop pushing each other to better, to higher."

Alaric nodded, looking serious. "I promise. Together, we shall explore the universe, between the sky and in hearts. We are each other's greatest adventure.

And when the first meteors flared across the sky, Lyra felt a flush of hope. The universe was vast, but she was no longer alone in it. Beside Alaric, she and her man loved to chase dreams, explore the world, and find gladness in the future. Together, they would write a story as endless as the stars above-filled with love, discovery, and new beginnings.